RICHARD H. ADAMS, JR.

MY BEST FRIEND CRAIG

To Leslie

CHAPTER 1

When I was older—much older—I could see where we went wrong. He was just too dominant, too self-possessed. We should have tried to rein him in. But how? Who exactly could tell Craig "no?" Certainly, his parents tried and failed. And so did the school vice-principal, Mr. Fagan. And the police. Probably the best person at restraining Craig was Danny. But Danny was only a kid, just like me. And Danny only succeeded on occasion.

You see, Craig was really headstrong. So strong that he could lead each of us around by our noses. At first, we kind of liked this: his crazy plans were so much fun. But each scheme made him bolder, and pretty soon he began mimicking some really unsavory characters. And then the house of cards that was Craig collapsed.

I have no desire here to put down Craig. He was, after all, my best friend during a really difficult time. I needed a friend, a best friend, and he needed a follower, or two or three. If I would have been a better best friend, I would have tried to hold him back. But I didn't and that is the whole of this story.

CHAPTER 2

Craig was fourteen, and I was only thirteen, so maybe that's the reason I really looked up to him. I was always taught to respect my elders. But Craig also had this easy and confident air about him that attracted friends like flies. Within minutes he could take charge of any group of boys, and start ordering them around. And they would love it. And among the girls he was just as poised as could be. I was way too quiet and intense to be like that. While he directed everyone around, I could only follow.

We started to hang out that first summer in 1963 when I'd just moved to town. My family was always relocating: two years in this place and then three years in the next. My mother used to say that my dad never saw a place that he didn't want to live in. So, I never got a chance to find a best friend before Craig. In all my previous stops I had only spot friends who were there one day and gone the next.

Craig and his family had always lived here. They were like founding fathers of the place—or at least that's the way it seemed to me. Craig knew, or seemed to know, everyone.

I'm not sure why he let me tag along. Maybe our mothers talked and decided that we'd be good for each other. At that age, I thought my mom arranged everything behind my back. My mom had a will of iron and directed us around like a field marshal. My dad was usually too busy with work to take much of an interest in our daily lives. He was always there to support me in sports, but that's about it.

Sports are probably how Craig and I met that first week of June. I had nothing to do, and so I began running off to the playground to play baseball. That's where Craig was a permanent fixture at shortstop. He was tall and blond, and so sure and quick on his feet that he could easily turn a darting ground ball into a double play. I, on the other hand, was usually assigned to guard the dandelions out in right field. In those early days I only had a fifty-fifty chance of catching anything hit my way.

"Hey, Sonny, why don't you practice at home?" asked Craig in his very first spoken words to me. "I bet that with a little work you could catch a fly ball."

Craig was encouraging like that. In the beginning I thought that he was just trying to be friendly. But later on, I decided that he was encouraging me (and others) to believe in some kind of grand notion he had of himself. Craig had this view of the world, with himself as the sun and the rest of us as rocks or asteroids revolving around him. We could either circle around Craig and follow him hither and yon on his many crazy schemes, or get lost. There was no in-between.

"Thanks, Craig. I'll try to get my dad to throw some balls to me at home."

My first reply to him was quite guarded. I didn't want to admit that I was already practicing by myself, throwing the ball up into the air fifty times a day. Or that my dad was also drilling me on the weekends. When you're thirteen there's only so much that you're willing to admit. Confessing the truth is hard enough at any age, and when you're a young teenager a lot remains unsaid.

Also, I didn't want to say much on that first day for fear of being mocked. In all the other places I'd lived, boys were always making fun of other boys: for how they looked or dressed or talked. Having a bad haircut or wearing the wrong shirt or pair of pants were always surefire ways to get put-down. And the put-downs really hurt. So, to protect myself, I usually tried to say as little as possible.

All of this made me a good listener. And maybe a good judge of people. Anyway, it's how I got my first insight into the character that was Craig.

One noontime three of us were walking home from the playground, proudly carrying our bats and gloves in hand. I forget where Craig was, maybe still back at the playground. Anyhow, I was there with his two closest buddies: Danny and Mike. Although we had just met, from what I could tell, these two guys seemed pretty normal. Danny was clearly the more assertive one: he loved nothing better than telling stories about Craig behind his back. Mike didn't say much, but had the kind of quick, penetrating eyes that suggested he was just sitting back, taking everything in.

"Have you heard the one about Craig hopping railroad cars?" chortled Danny.

"What do you mean, hopping railroad cars?" I asked. From the playground I had noticed a busy railroad line running through the town. But I hadn't been up to the tracks yet nor had I noticed anyone hanging around them.

"Well, you have to promise not to tell," said Danny, arching his eyebrows and turning to me with a grin. "Because it's supposed to be a secret. But last summer Craig and his friend Graham spent a couple of weeks trying to hop boxcars."

"No way," I protested.

"Yeah, they tried to get me and Mike to join in. But we wouldn't. It's too dangerous. Just think what would happen if you tried to hop a railroad car and fell off."

"And that's just what happened," chimed in Mike.

"What do you mean?"

"Well, it's a bit mysterious," continued Danny, clearly enjoying his role as chief rapporteur, "but this is what I think happened. The two of them were trying to hop a boxcar a short way out of town, and somehow Graham slipped and fell and twisted his ankle pretty badly. Craig couldn't move him so he left him lying by the track while he ran back into town, looking for help."

"And that's when Graham got caught," interjected Mike.

"Caught by who?" I asked.

"The railroad people who patrol the track," continued Danny. "They found Graham lying on the rocks right near the track. They put him in their truck, brought him back to the station, and started making a big stink about him being out on the railroad line. They were sure he was trying to hop trains. So, they called his parents and made them come pick him up. And then Graham got into big trouble. He ended up with a broken ankle and a month of being grounded at home."

"At least that's what Graham says," Mike added.

"What do you mean?" I asked, puzzled. "Do you mean that Craig has a different story?"

"Oh yeah," replied Danny, widening his grin. "Craig never wants to take blame for any of his adventures that screw up. So, he claims that Graham fell and broke his ankle while they were running up the rocky embankment to the tracks. He says that they weren't even trying to hop cars that day."

"Which is all a bunch of hooey," observed Mike. "Why else would the two of them be out on the tracks except trying to hop cars? It's not like people run along the railroad lines for fun."

"But what does Graham say?" I asked, trying to get to the bottom of all this.

"Oh, after he got into so much trouble with his parents, he refused to say anything about the whole thing. He got everyone to sign his cast but never said how he fell. And then he and his family moved away at Christmas time, so no one knows the real story."

"Well, what do you think happened?" I asked.

"Most likely, Craig's not telling the truth here," Danny said, with only the slightest hesitation. "It's just like him to do something crazy, get caught, and then run away leaving a buddy in the lurch. He likes having fun, and doing stupid stuff, but he sure doesn't like getting caught."

"Has he ever done anything like this to you?"

"No," added Mike, the pensive one. "But we try not to put ourselves in such a position."

CHAPTER 3

The next couple of weeks were kind of a blur. The four of us would meet at the playground about ten, play baseball, go home for lunch, and then head back to the playground in the afternoon. Craig, all five feet six and 120 pounds of him, was always the leader; he decided what we should do and when we should do it. He was, after all, a whole head taller than Danny, Mike, and me. And he had those piercing blue eyes that instantly dismissed you if you had any alternative thoughts. Not that I had any of those. I could think OK about school things, but when it came to social situations—well, I was just happy to let others do the planning. Playing baseball, Ping-Pong, or even walking through the woods throwing rocks at squirrels were all fine with me.

One summer morning about a month after we met, Craig decided that we really needed to do something different. "Something entirely new," is the way he put it. "Something we've never done before."

Craig was a confident, cocky son of a gun, and when he got an idea like this there was no holding him back. The more outlandish the plan, the more he grinned and pushed. Encouraging or compelling us to do new and bizarre things was somehow his way of demonstrating his power over us.

Now the park by our playground had a large open sewer pipe. The concrete pipe had no fencing or cover, and it ran horizontally under the ground for many city blocks. It was just large enough for a person to crawl into. It was also dark and smelly and had probably attracted generations of curious teenage boys.

"Do you guys see that pipe?" snickered Craig one day as we headed home from the playground. "That pipe is filled with rats, and it runs under the streets all the way to China."

"Aw, bullshit," replied Danny, the second-most self-possessed member of our group. "I'm sure that there aren't any rats or anything in there."

Danny was short and squat. He also had an engaging grin that would begin around the corners of his mouth before lighting up the rest of his whole face. Danny had two older brothers and so was not as easily duped as the rest of us. Anxious to assert his authority in a more indirect way, he would often mutter and complain behind Craig's back. And sometimes he would even try to push back on our leader's more outlandish schemes. Whenever Craig suggested something really out of this world, Danny would be the first to object. But after a couple of minutes he would usually smile, shrug his shoulders, and mutter, "Aw, what the hell." And then he'd rush off with the rest of us to carry out Craig's latest stunt.

"Yeah, well, do you want to bet on it?" pressed Craig, always determined to prove his alpha role. "I'll bet you ten dollars that if we climb into that pipe and walk half a mile, we'll see some rats."

"What'll you do if we see rats? I bet they bite."

"Well, I have my penknife with me. And I bet if we see any rats, you'll run and I'll have to deal with them," replied Craig a bit triumphantly. Craig was always quick thinking on his feet and more than capable of making things up on the fly.

"OK, you're on," replied Danny. "I'll bet you ten dollars that there aren't any rats in that pipe. And if there are, you'll be the first to run."

And so, the four of us headed off for the pipe. A small trickle of water was flowing out of the pipe, so when we started into it, we had to straddle the water with our legs and keep our heads and butts down. Craig the leader went first, with his penknife open and clenched firmly in his right hand. Danny went next, and then Mike and I brought up the rear.

"What happens if it starts to rain?" I yelled as we crept our way into the dark concrete pipe. "Will we get trapped?"

"Oh hell, don't be a fraidy-cat," replied Craig. "It's not going to rain. Didn't you see the sun out when we started?"

"The sun wasn't out when we left," muttered Danny, quietly under his breath. "It was actually kind of cloudy."

The pipe ran between manhole covers in the surrounding street. Each manhole cover had rain gutters that provided the only source of light in the dark hole. The manhole covers were set every fifty yards or so, and at every cover the pipe opened up into a small square underground cell. I was sure that all the rats and vermin in the pipe lived in those underground cells.

"Did you hear that? Did you hear that?" cried Craig as we approached the square cell under the first manhole cover. "All those little scurrying noises—they sounded just like rats running away."

Sure enough, when we reached the first underground cell, we saw clumps of twigs and trash and small branches that looked like nests for something. The piles sat in the four corners of the cell and looked like they'd been carefully arranged by some nasty critter.

"I'm going to wreck these nests so they won't come back!" Craig yelled as he kicked away at the piles of debris.

"Yeah, let's get rid of these horrible things," Danny shouted in support.

After destroying the nests, we continued working our way through the increasingly dark and foul-smelling pipe. The further we went, the wider we had to straddle with our feet because the small trickle of water in the pipe had turned into a steady stream. This slowed down our progress because we also had to keep our heads down to avoid hitting the low-hanging concrete ceiling. After about ten minutes of sloshing along we began seeing light from the next underground cell. But just as we entered the cell, we heard the crack of thunder outside.

"Hell! Did you hear that?" Danny yelled, with a sudden note of apprehension in his voice. "It's going to rain. We need to get out of here."

"I'm telling you," Craig shouted back, "it's not going to rain. Just follow me."

Now none of us liked this idea, especially after Danny hoisted himself up out of the gutter and confirmed that, indeed, it was beginning to rain. And we started hearing the steady sound of raindrops hitting the pavement above us.

"We need to get out of here, now, before we get trapped!" Danny cried, as he slipped back down into the pipe. He now seemed really worried and anxious to end this little expedition.

"What are you, a bunch of wussies?" Craig yelled, clearly exasperated with his main critic, Danny. "I'm telling you, it's not going to rain very much. So, we'll all be fine. Just follow me."

I looked at Danny, he looked at me, and Mike looked at his feet. All three of us felt more than a little concerned. If it rained hard, and the pipe filled up, how were we ever going to get out of this alive? But none of us wanted to be the first to break up this first great adventure. And since

Craig was so insistent, and sure of himself, well, we just bit the bullet and followed on.

As we headed off into the blackness towards the next underground cell, the stream of fetid water beneath our feet grew bigger and bigger. Pretty soon it was so wide that we could no longer straddle it with our feet. So, our socks and shoes got all wet and soaked. And then debris— cans and bottles and newspapers—started coming down with the water, smacking against our feet. And then twigs and branches and all kinds of other stuff came down the pipe. It was a dirty and ugly and horrible crawl through hell—and we couldn't even see where we were going! I was following Danny, and Danny was following Craig, and hopefully, Craig was headed to the next possible exit. But we couldn't see anything except a tiny speck of light way, way ahead of us.

Somewhere along this final crawl to daylight I began worrying about dying. *What would happen if the water in the pipe got so deep that there was no place to breathe? What would we do then? Would our bodies just float out?*

The water and debris were almost up to our chests by the time we reached the light of the third underground cell. And we were all soaked to the skin and downright miserable.

"Quick, pull yourselves out of the pipe," yelled Craig, just as soon as we reached the cell. "Climb on out through the gutter, and don't let anyone see you." I guess that our leader was worried about getting caught by the police.

One by one, we did just like our leader instructed. It was raining hard by the time the last of us, Mike, emerged all wet and bedraggled from the rain gutter.

"Shit, that wasn't any fun at all," Danny exclaimed, after we had all picked ourselves up and run away from the gutter. "In fact, it was a total disaster."

"Aw hell, it wasn't that bad," responded Craig, not at all willing to assume responsibility for any type of screwup. "Nobody got hurt. And didn't you get to see some entirely new things down there?"

"Are you kidding me?" shouted the normally unflappable Mike. "The only thing we saw down there was muck and filth. And it stunk!"

As we moved off away into the street, letting the hard rain wash some of the stink off our bodies, Danny suddenly turned and shouted at Craig: "And what about our bet? We never did see any rats down there. And if we didn't see rats, then I win the ten-dollar bet."

"Ah, you're full of shit," Craig shouted, cool as ice even though he was still covered with mud from head to foot. "I won the bet because there are rats all over the place down there. You saw their nests."

"I saw nests, but not a single rat. And no one else here saw a rat, either."

As the two of them began yelling back and forth about their stupid bet, I thought to myself, *This is completely insane. Here, the four of us almost drowned and yet the two of them are arguing about some idiotic ten-dollar bet. What is this world coming to?*

So ended our first adventure with Craig. All of us were filthy, but alive, and no one had gained or lost any money. Danny never won his bet because, well, no one ever won any bets against our leader. Craig was as tight with his reputation as he was with his money. Not only would Craig never admit to doing wrong, but he would also rather have killed his mother than fork over any dollar bills.

CHAPTER 4

While some might like to mutter about him behind his back, in person, Craig was a real charmer. With a flick of the switch, he could talk and butter up anyone he chose. Usually he put on the schmooze to get us to do one crazy stunt or the other. But when he wanted to, Craig could lay on the charm just for the sheer pleasure of doing so.

The first time I noticed this was on our way home one day from the playground. All four of us were there, arguing about how far we could hit a baseball.

"Of course, I can hit it the furthest," yelled Craig. "Don't you remember last Monday when I smacked it over the fence?"

"But that ball wasn't fair," countered Danny. "So how can you count that as a hit?"

"Ah bullshit, fair or foul," remonstrated Craig. "What difference does it make? When have you ever hit it that far?"

Just as our argument looked like it was going to turn into blows, we turned a corner, and there they were—twin girls about our age.

"Oh, Craig! How are you doing?" yelled the taller of the two, as she sidled up to the leader of our pack. "When are you gonna come over for a swim?"

"We had so much fun the last time you came over," added her sister.

"Yeah, we got the pool all cleaned so that our friends could come over."

Both girls were blondes with cute, teenage freckles. They had wide animated hazel eyes and easy smiles. And both of them had big grins for Craig.

"Oh heck, I don't know," replied Craig without missing a beat. "I'm pretty busy playing ball during the day and then watching TV at night. But maybe we can work something out."

I didn't know about Danny and Mike, but I was absolutely amazed by this exchange. Never in my life had girls my age invited me anywhere! In fact, I really couldn't remember the last time girls had ever even uttered a word to me! Whenever I saw a girl that I knew, I usually moved to the other side of the street. I was as afraid of girls as Craig seemed to be at ease with them.

"But hey, what have the two of you been up to this summer? Have you been to the beach yet?" Craig rambled on, crossing his arms across his chest and smiling broadly.

"No, we haven't," replied Nancy, the more talkative of the two. "We're going to Ocean City in two weeks."

"Ocean City. Wow, the beach there is so neat and I love going to the boardwalk at night. There are so many great shops along the boardwalk."

"Well, why don't you come with us to Ocean City sometime?" asked Nancy, eager, it seemed, to do anything with our leader.

"Oh, I don't know if my parents would let me," replied Craig, narrowing his grin slightly. This was the first time I had ever heard Craig mention his parents. Perhaps he didn't want to go or maybe just the directness of the question caught him a bit off-guard. But like a cat that always lands on its feet, he recovered quickly by adding, "I could always ask them. I'm sure they would let me go."

Anxious to enter the conversation, Susan, the other twin, shifted the topic by asking, "How about you, Craig? Are you going to Maine this year?"

"Oh, we're not going to Maine until August."

"But isn't it too cold to swim in the ocean up there?" continued Susan. "That's why we always like going to Ocean City. It's so hot down there in July."

And so, the easy banter continued back and forth between the three of them. They clearly enjoyed each other's company. And they also enjoyed talking about nothing: beach trips, mutual friends, and plans for the coming school year.

The other three of us—Danny, Mike, and I—never ventured a mumbling word. We just hung around on the sidewalk, pretending to be bored. Staring off into space and saying nothing was something I was pretty good at. And it seemed that Danny and Mike were also pretty accomplished at this too.

Eventually, Nancy, noticing our discomfort, pointed towards the three of us wallflowers and asked: "Are these your friends, Craig?"

"Yeah, we all play ball down at the playground," replied Craig quickly, without offering to do any introductions. It was like he was embarrassed by our presence.

"Do they have names?" pressed Nancy, who was, it seemed, a rather self-possessed young girl.

"Oh yeah, they are Danny, Mike, and Sonny," replied our leader, looking rather miffed that he now had to admit our existence.

"Well, I recognize Danny and Mike," said Nancy. "But I don't think I've ever seen Sonny."

"Oh, he's new here," Craig said rapidly, without giving me a chance to open my trap. "He just moved here from Virginia."

"Well, nice to meet you," said Nancy, flashing me a quick grin. "I hope that you enjoy hanging around with Craig. He'll keep you busy and entertained, that's for sure."

"Thanks," I replied, without daring to ask her what "busy and entertained" might mean.

Girls were just too new for me to want to press my luck.

CHAPTER 5

As the summer wore on, we began spending more time out in the woods. In our area the woods were dark and deep, and ran north and south along several fast-flowing creeks and streams. They also followed along the sides of the busy commuter railroad line that had gotten Craig and Graham into so much trouble before. We often crossed this railroad line in our wanderings to see how far north we could hike without being seen. We liked to pretend that we were modern-day Indians, trying to travel as far as we could through the trees without being detected by pale-faced settlers.

"Hey," cried Craig in a eureka-like moment one listless summer afternoon. "How about if we try hiking along the railroad to Philly?" Philadelphia was the closest major city and the end point for the commuter line. I'd only been to Philadelphia once, when I went with my dad to buy some new shoes. It didn't seem like a place where I wanted to spend time; I much preferred hanging out with my buddies.

"Oh no!" yelled Danny almost immediately. "That would be about twenty miles; that's way too far to hike. Also, walking along the railroad ties is too hard. It's a lot easier just walking through the woods."

While Danny was almost as adventurous as Craig, he was far more practical. Craig was always dreaming up something wild that Danny would try to cut back to size. But through sheer persistence, Craig would almost invariably get his way. He would conjure up something incredible, and then work and work on it until we were at least half-way persuaded. And then he would smile his little smile, and press us a bit more until we caved in. Craig's leadership was like that: easy for the most part but quite determined for the really crazy things that he decided just *had* to be done.

I have no idea why Craig decided that we *needed* to hike to Philly. We had never talked about Philly, and there was no particular place in the city that any of us wanted to visit. Probably he decided on Philly because it was off there shimmering in the distance and it presented a new kind of challenge for his leadership. Craig loved challenges, and he liked pushing the three of us to go out and meet them.

While no one bothered to ask, I personally didn't care one way or another about this new brainstorm. Hiking to Philly seemed difficult, but at least it would be something new to do. So, Craig just had to whittle away at Danny's objections to his scheme. And that didn't take too long, given Craig's ability to direct us around.

Mike wasn't there the afternoon that Craig announced his plan, but when he heard about it, he quickly announced that he was "unavailable." Mike was like that: as the youngest and smallest member of our gang, he was not very adventurous. He was an only child with an overprotective mother, so sometimes he just decided to stay home. Try as we might, we could never persuade Mike to join us once he'd opted to stay put. He was very stubborn that way.

A couple of days later Craig, Danny, and I headed north along the railroad track to Philly. Each of us had packed a small lunch that we had prepared on the sly. None of us wanted our parents to know about this expedition; we all figured that the less our parents knew, the better. On the hike I carried an old Boy Scout backpack to hold our lunches. We weren't worried about water, because we figured we could drink Indian-style out of one of the streams along the way.

It was a hot, humid day without a breath of wind, and so we were quickly covered with sweat. Clambering over the rocks and ties in the railroad bed was just as difficult as Danny had predicted.

"This stinks," Danny yelled, always anxious to show that he'd been right in the first place. "How are we ever going to walk twenty miles like this?"

"Hell, don't complain," replied Craig. "It'll get better when we get used to this kind of hiking."

"But what happens when a train comes along?"

"When a train comes along," assured our leader, "we'll just duck off into the woods. That should be easy."

And it was in fact easy when the first eight-car train came flying by, honking its horn at us as it rounded a curve. At that moment we were on a slightly raised embankment, and we only had to scoot down into the woods to let the train pass by.

But Craig evidently didn't like this arrangement. And so, when the next train came by, he stayed up on the embankment. Ignoring the loud air horn of the conductor, Craig stood planted just a few feet away from the speeding locomotive.

"Hey, check this out," he cried, evidently quite pleased with himself. "The wind from the train really cools you off. And it's neat to stand so close to a moving train."

I didn't like this particular dare at all. It seemed dangerous and foolish. *Why risk your life for such a dumb trick?* I thought. But when the third train whooshed by, Danny joined Craig. The two of them stood on the embankment only a couple of paces away from the hurtling train. They just covered their ears and laughed out loud when the conductor really laid on his horn.

"Hey, Sonny!" shouted Danny as the train sped away. "This is super neat. You need to join us up here next time. It's really thrilling."

"OK; I'll think about it," I said.

But I didn't move a muscle to join them the next time a train flew by. I was just too scared to join in such craziness.

Pretty soon we came to our first railroad trestle. This bridge was about thirty yards above the ground and stretched for fifty or so yards across a small muddy creek.

"What do we do now?" I asked. "There's not nearly enough space on the side for all of us to walk across. And what happens if a train comes when we're out on the bridge?"

"No problem," cried the ever-confident Craig. "I'll run across first, and then each of you can follow. We're fast and should be able to make it across before any trains come."

"OK," replied Danny, clearly up for the challenge.

I said nothing and felt a knot slowly rising in my stomach. Running across a bridge with a train headed at your rear end wasn't my idea of fun.

Fortunately, the track here was straight in both directions, so we'd be able to see any train well before it approached. Feeling that I should contribute something, I shouted, "Do you want me to look up and down the track and give you an all-clear signal, Craig?"

But before I could finish my sentence, Craig took off running over the trestle. He made it in good time, and when he reached the end, he turned around, waved at us, and began laughing. He was having the time of his life!

Danny went next; I gave him the backpack to carry because I was the slowest. Danny also made it easily and joined our leader in giggles at the other side. The two of them obviously loved facing down danger.

When it was my turn, I looked both ways, said a prayer, and ran as fast as I could. I made it but was scared as the dickens the entire way. It seemed like it would be very easy to die out there on that bridge. At the end I felt more like crying than smiling.

"How about if we dip down into the woods now?" I pleaded. "We can get out of the sun and walk in the woods right next to the tracks. That will be a lot cooler and faster."

"No way," responded Craig. "It's a lot more fun trying to race the trains. And I'm sure that it's faster following the tracks, because they're more direct."

So, we continued walking down the railroad line until it was time for lunch. At this point Craig relented and we dropped down into the dark, green woods to eat our peanut butter and jelly sandwiches. We washed our sandwiches down by getting down on our knees and slurping out of one of the streams.

"How much further do you think we have to go?" Danny asked.

"I bet that it's another fifteen miles to Philadelphia," replied Craig.

"But that's way too far," I objected. "I need to be home by five." Since it was now about one, that gave us maybe four more hours of walking.

"Aw, don't worry," said our leader. "We'll be back by then. But next time we need to start earlier so that we can make it all the way to Philly."

We spent the next hour or so working our way down the railroad. The sun continued to beat down, but no trains passed. We were probably in the midafternoon lull between the morning and evening commutes.

Eventually we came to our second railroad trestle. This one spanned a much larger creek or, more accurately, stream. The bridge was about eighty yards long and maybe forty yards above the wide and rapidly moving stream. This bridge had even less room on the sides than the first one. In fact, there really was no room on the sides at all; the wooden railroad ties just ended, and then there was nothing but air.

"Wow, guys, this looks like fun," cried Craig enthusiastically. "We'll do it just like we did the last. I'll run across first, and then you guys follow."

Craig clearly relished this daredevil challenge. And it *was* a daredevil challenge, because the run here was much longer and the train track wasn't straight at all. The track here made a long, slow right turn before the bridge and then a quick left turn after the bridge, so it was impossible to see more than fifty yards down the line in either direction.

I didn't like the last crossing, and this bridge was twice as long and frightening. So, I did my best to protest. "Craig, this doesn't look very safe. You can't see very far down the track in either way. A train could come up on us really fast."

"Aw, don't be a killjoy. Everything will be fine. We'll just run faster."

"And what choice do we have?" chimed in Danny. "We can't exactly give up and turn around."

Craig shot a quick approving glance at Danny before briefly looking up and down the track. And then he set off like a bullet down the middle of the line. But just as soon as he got twenty yards down the track, Danny and I heard, and then spotted, a commuter train coming our way. We couldn't really tell how fast it was moving. But it sure looked like it was traveling a whole lot faster than our leader was running.

"Craig, run!" we both yelled at the top of our lungs. "There's a train coming!"

Craig turned and spotted the train. A look of instant panic welled up in his eyes, and he started running for his life. His arms began pumping up and down, and his legs started churning like an Olympic sprinter's. Still, he was no match for the train, which began blowing its air horn continuously.

About two-thirds of the way over the railroad trestle, Craig apparently realized that it was hopeless. After a quick backward glance, he veered suddenly to the right and fell to his knees next to the rails. In a flash he grabbed one of the wooden railroad ties and lowered himself down until his whole body was dangling off the bridge. About ten seconds later the train zoomed by as he hung suspended in midair below the bridge.

All of this happened in a flash. First Craig was running, and then he was holding on to the trestle for dear life. I couldn't believe what I was seeing. *What a horrible way to die*, is all I could think.

"Help!" screamed Craig at the top of his lungs. "Help me get up!"

The two of us raced to where he was dangling in midair. Each of us grabbed an arm and hauled him back up to the railroad track. Craig seemed to be totally spooked; his face was white and strained, his hands were shaking, and his eyes were as big as saucers. And for once he was speechless—not that any of us wanted to talk. Just as soon as we pulled him up, the three of us ran like hell to get off the bridge.

"Damn, that was close!" Craig panted, just as soon as he'd caught his breath. "That train came up a lot faster than I ever thought was possible."

"It sure did!" Danny hollered. "You're lucky to be alive." Danny's eyes seemed almost as large as our leader's.

"The next time I run across a bridge," Craig continued, without paying the slightest attention to Danny, "I'm going to make double sure that nothing is coming before I start. That was just too scary."

"You're going to do that again?" I yelled, not believing what I had just heard. "You almost got killed! Why would you ever want to do that again?"

"Yeah, why would you ever want to do that again?" echoed Danny.

Craig looked at both of us for a moment or two before softly replying, "Oh, you guys just don't understand. I love physical challenges, and that was like the challenge of all challenges."

"But it was a stupid challenge that could've got you killed!" Danny screamed.

"Oh, I don't know," mused our leader. "I knew what I was doing the whole time. I just need to be more careful about when I start to run, that's all."

"You had absolutely no idea what you were doing!" yelled Danny, still clearly upset and sure that Craig was just trying to put up a brave front.

"You're nuts—completely nuts—and you're going to get yourself killed," is all I could muster.

After this the three of us abandoned our hike to Philly. On the way back we started very slowly and crossed the two trestles with a lot more respect. On the longer trestle, Danny went down to the end of the curve and gave us the "all clear" signal for each of us to dart across. On the shorter trestle we looked around each and every way before running one by one across the bridge.

On our whole way home Danny did most of the talking and directing; Craig was strangely subdued the entire time. But he must have been replaying in his mind everything that had happened, because about halfway back he suddenly blurted out, "You know, that was fun! Not the kind of fun that I would want to do every day, but it was a really scary and awesome kind of fun."

"But how could it be fun to almost get killed?" I shouted again.

"Sonny, you just don't understand—I wasn't that close to dying. I knew what I was doing the whole time."

"Craig, you're crazy," I replied.

CHAPTER 6

Among the boys I knew, Craig was certainly a natural and self-assured leader. He could take and lead the four of us anywhere. But we were definitely not the coolest kids in town, and there were certainly other confident leaders around. After all, we were only eighth graders, and everyone knew that ninth graders ruled. We were also by and large "good boys," and everyone knew that the bad boys moved to a whole different tune. And it was the bad boys who controlled our town.

Or at least that's the way it seemed to me anytime Todd was around. Todd was a tall, strapping, wide-shouldered fifteen-year-old who wore the thickest black glasses imaginable. While he always had a goofy kind of smile, Todd was certainly not one to mess with. He was at least three inches taller and thirty pounds heavier than anyone else around. At the playground he could lift and bench press twice as much as any other eighth or ninth grader. And his biceps were the talk of all the boys. He was like a fifteen-year-old Mr. Universe.

Whenever Todd appeared at the playground, Craig would grow very subdued. He would shrink into himself: no more loud remonstrating or boasting or crazy shenanigans. He would almost become like a normal boy.

There was definitely a weird kind of dynamic between Craig and Todd. Todd was much bigger and stronger than our leader, but he lacked Craig's charisma. Todd got his way by physical force or the threat of physical force; Craig got people to follow more by the aura of his personality. Whenever Todd was around, Craig would silently give in to his lead, but not without a kind of "Watch out, I told you so" look on his face. Craig always seemed sure that something bad would happen anytime Todd was around. And he was usually right.

While the boys in our gang were interested in sports, Todd was not much of an athlete. He was always more interested in pranks and getting into trouble than playing any kind of ball game. He was the one who would egg strangers' cars at night, just because it was fun. Or steal things off grocery shelves or let the air out of people's tires. Todd was accomplished at all these nefarious tricks. When he was younger, one of his favorite pranks was riding his bike and lifting sandwiches and soda off the local lunch truck. Some people said that he was wild because his parents were divorced and his dad lived out of town. Others said that he was a troublemaker because he was so much bigger and stronger than everyone else. And a few people said that he was just plain born bad.

Somehow Todd heard about our adventure on the railroad trestle. I don't know how he learned about it, because none of us ever talked to him. Following Craig's lead, we did our best to avoid him.

Todd liked to stir up trouble, especially among younger kids. And so, the next time he spotted us on the playground, he hollered, "Hey, guys! I heard that you had some fun out on the train tracks the other day."

"Nah," replied Craig quickly. "It wasn't that much fun. We were just out hiking along the railroad line."

"Well," pressed Todd, "if you want to have some real fun on the tracks, you should follow me some afternoon—that is, if you're not too scared."

Todd's reputation was a bad one, and so I was sure that his notion of "real fun" was probably very different from ours. I figured to myself that if he thought his plan was "fun," then it was certainly way over the top for me. I'm not sure what Craig thought: he always seemed a bit mesmerized by Todd. But I think that Danny felt just like me.

Unfortunately for us, Todd was nothing if not persistent. Every time he saw us at the playground over the next two weeks, he renewed his dare. And he would call us "chickens" or "girlie girls" or worse for not following his lead.

One day at the playground, Craig suddenly gave into Todd's taunting. To this day I really have no idea why he caved in. Without a doubt Todd's mocking was something new to Craig, because no one had ever taunted our leader. It was usually Craig who did all the badgering. So, Craig definitely felt put out by Todd's behavior and wanted it to end. Probably Craig was also anxious to demonstrate that no one could push him around: he was just as tough as anyone. But it's also likely that Craig was just plain curious to see what this bad boy had in mind. After all, Craig loved challenges, and Todd represented all kinds of new and twisted challenges. The only problem is that most of these challenges were bad.

"OK, we'll go with you," Craig said with a long sigh, as if he'd been wrestling with this decision for a long time. "But whatever you want us to do, it can't be dangerous, or else we just won't do it."

Craig was certainly speaking in the royal "we" here, because Danny and I hadn't said a word. Danny would sometimes question Craig's initiatives, but he would become quite mute whenever Todd was around. Craig respected Todd, but Danny and I were just plain scared of him.

"Don't worry, it won't be dangerous," assured Todd. "Just follow me to the station in town, and I'll show you what's up."

The four of us headed to the railroad station, from where we turned south along the track to where it crossed a seldom-used back road. A short way below the road and off the railroad embankment, Todd pointed to a partly covered manhole cover out in the woods.

"OK, guys, here's what we're going to do," instructed our new leader. "I'm going to screw this manhole cover off, and then you guys are going to help me carry it up and over to the railroad tracks. Then we'll put it on the track and wait for the next train to come along and slice the cover in half."

"Shit!" cried Craig, suddenly looking very worried. "That's dangerous as hell! Are you really sure that the train can cut it in half?"

"Damn yes—of course I'm sure."

"Have you ever done this before?" Craig pressed.

"Sure," replied Todd. "Grant and me have done this a bunch of times."

"Grant? He's a hoodlum!" yelled Danny, abruptly coming to life. "My brother says that he's in reform school now."

Since this was the first time I'd ever heard anyone mention reform school, I figured that this Grant—whoever he was—must be a *really* bad boy. *We're moving in some really shaky company here*, I thought to myself.

"Aw hell," Todd growled. "Don't believe everything you hear." Flashing Danny a very irritated look, he added, "Grant's a good guy. And what does your brother know anyways?"

Stunned back into silence, Danny had no reply.

"Now, are you guys just going to stand there and give me lip?" Todd said, seizing the initiative again. "Or are you going to help?"

We watched while this young Mr. Universe strained to get the heavy, cast-iron manhole cover off. Screwing it off was something that I never would have dreamed about doing in a million years. But Todd was very strong and determined. After about fifteen minutes of huffing and puffing, he finally succeeded.

"Phew, that was a lot of work," he announced, prying the round cover off its housing. "Now you guys have to help me roll and carry it over to the tracks. I sure can't do that by myself. It must weigh five hundred pounds."

So, the four of us rolled the huge cover about twenty-five yards over to the side of the railway embankment. From there we somehow managed to lug it up to the level of the tracks. Todd did most of the work here; while he held and carried half the iron cover, the three of us struggled to support the other half.

"This is heavy as hell!" Craig yelled as we approached the top of the hill. "Can't we put it down to rest?"

"No, don't be a sissy," Todd shot right back. "Don't put it down until we're all the way up. It's way too heavy to pick up again."

At the top of the embankment, Todd had us roll the cover over so that it rested on just one of the railroad tracks.

"You can't lay it on both rails," he explained. "Because that would derail the train."

"Are you sure about all this?" asked a clearly worried Craig. "Even with that thing on only one rail, it sure looks like it'll knock the train off the track."

"Aw, shut up," hissed Todd. "I've got this all figured out. Like I've told you, I've done this a hundred times before. Just let me do all the thinking here and everything will be OK. You guys just sit back and watch."

And so, watch we did. We ran over to the woods, crouched down in the bushes, and waited. I remember thinking to myself, *Here it is a beautiful summer day, and we're just sitting waiting to see a train wreck. And for people to die.*

We didn't have to wait very long. Pretty soon an eight-car train came flying along and *BOOM!* It hit our manhole cover. We heard the deafening sound of metal smashing metal and saw pieces of steel flying everywhere. From inside the train, we could hear people yelling and screaming and crying.

The locomotive leaped into the air for a brief microsecond and then shot off the track. The locomotive and the front two cars went screeching down the embankment, overturning as they barreled off into the trees. The rest of the cars slammed into one another, piling up like a stack of twisted dominoes off the track.

At the sight of the locomotive flying off the tracks, we took off sprinting through the woods. Following Todd, we ran like madmen trying to put as much distance as possible between ourselves and the wrecked train. We ran in a zigzag through the woods so that no one could follow us. And we didn't stop running until we reached the playground some fifteen minutes later.

"What the hell!" screamed Craig, just as soon as we'd stopped and caught our breath. "I thought you said that you'd done this before and that the train had never derailed? What the hell happened this time?"

"I don't know," snarled Todd right back. "I've done this before with Grant, and the train has never gone off the track. I don't know what happened."

Craig, Danny, and I were as scared as could be. Craig's and Danny's eyes were as big as they were that time on the railroad trestle. And I was shaking from head to foot. To think that we had caused a train full of passengers to run off its track was simply unbelievable. None of us had ever done anything like this in our whole entire lives! How would we ever explain this to anyone?

But Todd, weird prankster that he was, didn't seem all that upset. He wasn't at all nervous and he still had that goofy half-smile plastered on his face. And his eyes looked like they always did: shifty and unreadable behind those thick bottle-like glasses. Truth be told, Todd actually seemed to enjoy being in the eye of a disaster that he had created.

"Look, guys," he said, anxious to take charge. "Don't breathe a word about this to anyone! I'm sure no one got hurt, and pretty soon everyone will forget that this ever happened. But you've got to keep your mouths closed. Do you hear me?"

"Yes," we nodded in unison, since we knew we had no choice. If we talked, and our parents found out, we'd be in big trouble. They would call the police and the cops would haul us in for questioning. And then we'd be sent to reform school or jail. Or worse. But if we zipped our lips and stayed quiet, maybe nothing would happen. No one would be the wiser, and after a while everyone would forget.

"But what should we do if anyone asks us about it?" ventured Danny in a very quiet voice.

"Just play dumb and don't say anything," warned Todd, holding a single finger up to his lips. "If you talk, you'll get into trouble with your parents *and* the cops. And then you'll have to deal with me."

In situations like this, Todd could be awfully convincing. And intimidating.

The next day, we read in the newspaper that one man had been killed and five people seriously injured in the derailment. The dead man was a passenger, a middle-aged commuter, who was sitting by an open window in the second car. When the car flew off the track and overturned, he'd sailed through the window and died on the embankment.

Craig, Danny, and I were devastated. None of us had ever been involved in an accident before, let alone one that had killed someone and had left five people critically injured. *How could we have done something like this?* I thought. *Why did we ever listen to that crazy hooligan Todd? How could we have been so stupid?*

We had absolutely no idea of what to do. We knew that the accident was a dumb and stupid prank that had gone horribly wrong. One innocent person had died, someone we could never bring back. We should never, ever have been part of such a crazy and terrible thing. We had listened to a really bad boy, and it was his harebrained scheme that had led to such an awful outcome. But how should we get out of this dreadful mess? If we talked, Todd would certainly come looking for us; he was definitely strong and mean enough to beat all three of us up. And the police, well, that was just too dreadful to even think about. We were probably too young to go to jail, but how many eighth graders had killed someone? Maybe they had a special kind of prison for eighth grade murderers!

Paralyzed by fear, we did nothing. Absolutely nothing. We just moped around and worried ourselves sick.

Maybe we should have tried to see Todd. But Danny and I had always been petrified by this menacing boy-man. And by now, even Craig seemed scared of him. We also began hearing strange and conflicting stories about his whereabouts. Some said that Todd had left town in order to go live with his dad. Others said that his mom, finally fed up with all his dumb escapades, had packed him off to military school. A few even claimed that he'd fled to Canada. In any event, we never saw him again at the playground. And he was not in our junior high when school started in September.

CHAPTER 7

It took us a long time to recover from this tragedy. For the first two weeks, Craig, Danny, and I lived in constant fear of the police appearing suddenly at our door. We stopped going to the playground and just hung around at home waiting for the inevitable. I think that I suffered more than the others. I was sure that every knock at the door or call on the phone was the cops.

As the days passed and nothing happened, we decided to take steps to cover our tracks. We stopped talking about the accident at all. If we had to refer to it among ourselves, we called it "the event." And we never breathed a word about the accident to anyone else, even to our buddy Mike. When others would bring it up, we'd either grow silent or try to change the subject.

I know that the police went around town trying to find out how the manhole cover came to rest on the track. And I'm pretty sure that they went to call on Todd. After all, he was the leading prankster in town. Everyone knows that manhole covers just don't pick themselves up and go lie down on railroad tracks. Todd was the perfect suspect for doing such a dastardly deed.

But Todd had probably left town by the time the police went looking for him. Todd was good at disappearing, especially when he was wanted by the law. He probably even had a couple of escape routes already planned. In any event, the three of us never heard anything about the details of the police investigations. The cops were always calling on older boys and those with bad reputations. I was too new to the community to draw any suspicion. And Craig and Danny were commonly viewed as "good boys"; not at all the type of hoodlum to be involved in such an awful disaster.

In early September, Craig decided that we had to do something new and different to try to forget our troubles. Football was now in the air with all the local teams beginning to practice before school began. Unfortunately, we were all still too young to play on the school team; that didn't start until the ninth grade. So, Craig decided to organize a tackle football game on the grandest possible scale. He decided to assemble a whole horde of us—fifteen or so boys without helmets, pads, or any other type of protection—and play what he dubbed "a football game for the ages" in the park. He thought that this would be the perfect way to forget our problems and end the summer with a bang.

Now, my family—or, more specifically, my mother—had strictly forbidden me to play tackle football. As a strict rules' follower, she was convinced that football was only a game for juvenile delinquents. According to her, playing football could only lead to smashed heads, broken bones, or worse. Time and time again she told me that her brother had broken his leg playing tackle football, and that he still walked with a limp. The only problem with this story is that it wasn't quite true. On the few occasions when I met my uncle, I never noticed any kind of limp. And he never made reference to any football-related injury. My mom was always telling me stories aimed at improving my behavior. The only hitch was that some of these stories didn't exactly match reality.

Because of my mother's strong feelings, I never played any football in her presence. But when I was out of her sight, I always played tackle football. In fact, that was the only kind of football I ever played. It was my favorite game. I guess I figured that whatever my mom didn't know wouldn't hurt her.

Craig, being the quick and sure-footed athlete that he was, also loved tackle football. He always wanted to play quarterback: the one getting the ball first and making all the decisions. He wanted to be able to pass the ball to a receiver flying down the sidelines, or to tuck the ball to his side and race up the field to the cheers of everyone in the stands. Craig was shifty and fast, so with a head fake here and a hip move there, he could usually beat everyone to the goal. In the end zone he would slam down the ball, yell out, clap his hands, and do a little wiggle dance with his hips. Craig was definitely a showboat, and the football field provided him with the perfect stage to show off his many skills.

On the last Saturday before school began, fourteen of us assembled in the wide, grassy park by the playground. The park was the perfect place for such an epic game. It stretched forever and was divided down the middle by a small creek. This was the same creek that flowed out of the sewer drain that we'd explored in June. With the creek as the sideline on one side and the road on the other, we marked off two end zones with small orange cones.

Once we all arrived, Craig promptly took charge. "We need to choose up teams," he announced. "So, Tom and I will pick sides. Tom, you go first."

Tom was an entirely new face to me; I'd never seen him at the playground. He had thick brown hair and was about five feet six: just as tall as Craig. However, Tom was a bit stockier than our leader, weighing maybe 130 pounds or so. Much of his weight seemed to be concentrated in his wide and powerful-looking shoulders. I thought to myself that if Tom could run, then he would be a very difficult guy to bring down. I was always worrying about tackling the big, fleet-footed players.

Tom and Craig selected the teams. Craig chose Danny with his second pick; although he was short, Danny was fast and a sticky-fingered pass receiver. Tom chose me fourth. I was happy because several boys—mostly smaller and younger boys—were selected after me.

I always hated the process of choosing teams. My worst dreams at night usually featured me being the very last person to be chosen for a baseball or football team. It was so unfair. I thought to myself, *I'm not that bad. If only the captains knew how hard I'll try, then they'd <u>never</u> choose me last.*

We kicked off to Craig's team. Craig caught the kickoff and squirmed and weaved his way halfway up the sixty-yard field before being tackled en masse. He bounded up and immediately began playing quarterback. He clearly loved ordering his players about and drawing up plays on his hands or in the dirt. Since he knew Danny so well, he made him one of his receivers.

I wasn't fast, and so Tom told me to play defensive line. The other boys who joined me there were either fat or slow. The fat boys were good at bulling their way to the quarterback, while the slow boys—well, that was just the only place for us to play. All the speedy boys, like Tom, played in the back defending against Craig's passes.

At first there was a lot of confusion about how and when we on the defensive line could rush the quarterback. Craig again took over. "OK, you guys on defense," he said, motioning toward me, "you can't rush the passer until you count to ten. And you have to count slowly, like 'one-potato, two-potato,' until ten. When you reach ten, you can go after the quarterback."

The three of us on the defensive line didn't like this rule one little bit. We would've much preferred to rush the quarterback right away so that we could bring him down and earn a little glory. But how could we object? This was Craig's game, and he was setting all the rules. We had no say.

"Also, the only way you get a first down is by completing three passes," added our leader. "Otherwise, no first downs."

Craig probably included this rule because he thought that he was the only one on the field who could complete three straight passes.

Despite his very high opinion of himself, Craig and his team went nowhere in its first set of downs. Danny dropped the first pass that he threw, and one of my teammates tackled Craig as he tried to run on the second play. Their third play also went nowhere. So, Craig's team had to punt.

Our leader, Tom, fielded the kick, ran up the sideline away from the creek, and was quickly tackled. Since he could throw a good and accurate spiral, Tom became our quarterback. He was a confident and take-charge leader—almost as cocky as Craig. He promptly assigned each of us positions on offense.

Tom completed his first three passes, and we got a first down. However, I didn't get to see any of this action. Tom had assigned me to play the very unglamorous position of center. Obviously, someone had to snap the ball to the quarterback. But between having my head down to hike the ball and then trying to block the people who were rushing, I could barely see what was happening anywhere on the field. I quickly decided that I was just there to block and tackle for the speedy ones, like Tom and Craig. They got all the glory because they were the only ones who could score touchdowns.

Our drive soon stalled, and we had to punt. Craig fielded the punt and started up the sideline by the creek. He easily outran the first wave of tacklers. I was in the second wave, and he was about ready to juke and run by me. In a moment of desperation, I dove at his knees, and he jumped awkwardly into the air trying to avoid me. One of Craig's feet caught my shoulder, and he landed upside down on his arm in the dirt by the side of the creek.

"Aw hell!" he yelled, grabbing his left arm. "My arm hurts. In fact, it hurts like hell."

Craig sat up slowly and showed us his left arm. He couldn't move it and had to hold it carefully with his other arm.

"Shit," he continued. "Look at it! It's all black and blue and starting to swell."

Sure enough, when we peered down at his arm, it was beginning to swell. But we couldn't see any bone or anything poking through. However, when Danny reached out to touch it, Craig screamed again, "Shit, stay away! It hurts too much."

For a boy who never feared anything, Craig was in real pain. I'd never, ever seen him like this.

"What are you going to do?" someone asked.

"Hell, I have to go home. My arm hurts so much I can't even bend it! I bet I'm going to have to go to the doctors."

Two of us helped Craig stand up. Cussing loudly, and fighting back tears, he started on home, gingerly cradling his left arm with his right.

"Do you want me to come with you?" offered Danny, anxious to help.

"Nah, I'll make it," replied our leader. Proud as ever, Craig wanted to make it on his own.

A sudden gloom descended upon the rest of us as we watched Craig slowly trudge away.

"Hell, we can't play without Craig," declared Tom, just as soon as our leader was beyond earshot. "There's no one else to play quarterback for the other team."

No one spoke up to challenge this. Even Danny, who had a fine arm and could really throw a football, stayed mum.

"And anyhow," added Tom, "it was Craig's game in the first place."

The rest of us had nothing to say. We stood around awkwardly for a while wondering what to do. Then we began picking up the orange cones. Tom was right: without our playmaker and organizer, none of us wanted to continue playing. Our much-anticipated grand finale to summer was over before it even got going.

And it was all my fault! I was the only tackler; no one else was around when Craig jumped and fell. So, all the blame fell on me. I felt terrible. I was probably the worst thirteen-year-old on the field, and yet I'd knocked out our best player. *How could I have done such a thing?* I asked myself over and over again.

None of the other boys had anything to say to me as we walked on home. But I knew what they were all thinking: "How could this useless bloke knock out Craig?"

In the awkward silence I started worrying about what my parents would do. What would they say when they heard that I'd been playing tackle football *and* that I'd broken Craig's arm? This time there was no way to bottle up the bad news. Sooner or later Craig's mother and my mother were bound to talk, and then all hell would break loose. I would be lucky to ever get out of the house again!

About a week later our mothers did indeed talk, and all of heaven's fury descended on me. My father cuffed me about the ears and whipped me with a belt on my backside, and then my mom sent me to bed without dinner. I was also forced to apologize to both Craig and his mom over the phone. And then I was grounded for a whole month.

Craig missed the first week of school, so I didn't see him again until the beginning of the second week. Although we were in the same grade, we weren't in the same classes or even in the same section of classes. So, it wasn't until one morning in the halls before the first bell rang that I suddenly bumped into him.

"Hey, man," he greeted me, with that warm and effusive smile. "How are you doing? Any news about the event?"

"No, I haven't heard anything," I replied. "No one has said anything to me about it at all. And you? Have you heard anything?"

"No, I haven't heard anything, either. No one has come calling at my house. I guess that's good."

"And how's your arm?" I asked, trying to shift topics.

"I'm fine. Look at my cast. Everyone's been signing it."

I'd heard through the grapevine that Craig had been lining up the girls to sign his cast. His injury had made him quite famous among members of the opposite sex. I'm sure that Craig loved his newfound celebrity.

"Do you want to sign it?" he asked with a grin.

"Nah, I need to get to class."

"Hey, you know what?" yelled Craig, as I tried to slither away without assuming any more responsibility for his injury. "You just might become a good defensive player on the football team."

"Thanks, Craig," I said, beaming a bit on the inside. There was nothing that I wanted more than to be a part of a real football team. But that would have to wait until I was in ninth grade.

CHAPTER 8

About ten days later things took a big change for the worse. The vice principal of our junior high called the three of us into a meeting. We weren't the only ones summoned; four or five other boys warily shuffled into the midmorning meeting. I knew two of these boys by reputation only, and their reputations were not good.

Mr. Fagan was the vice principal at our school. He was the big, stern, no-nonsense head of all things related to discipline. Rumor had it that he loved to paddle wayward boys and give them after-school detention. People also said that he enjoyed suspending the really bad boys from school. According to everyone, he was a man to be avoided at all costs.

On that morning we had no choice as we marched in to meet Mr. Fagan. Peering down on each of us through his thick, horn-rimmed glasses, he motioned for us to take seats around a conference table. He wasted no time on flowery introductions. "Boys, you've all been called into this meeting today because we think that you might know something about that terrible train wreck last month. The police have asked us to talk to you and see if you can provide us with any useful information. I'm sure you all know that one man died and five were seriously injured in that accident."

None of us responded to this opening salvo. I glanced at Craig, he looked at Danny, and Danny stared at the floor. The other boys squirmed around uncomfortably in their seats. I thought to myself, *Here it is, just like in the movies. They're going to press and squeeze us until we pop out with the truth. And then we're all going to jail.*

"Now come on, boys," urged Mr. Fagan, anxious to break the stony silence. "There's no reason to be afraid. If you know anything about this accident, it's your duty to speak up. You won't get into any trouble for telling the truth."

To emphasize the gravity of the matter, Mr. Fagan began his favorite staring routine. One by one he peered carefully and intently at each of us arrayed around the table. No doubt he thought that if he fixed his mean, stony stare on each of us long enough, someone would blurt out something.

But again no one volunteered a word. I began studying a small hole in the wall, right where a pipe ran through a baseboard in the floor. I started wondering how I could slither down, squeeze through that hole, and run on home.

"How about you, Craig?" asked the vice principal, abandoning the baleful stare for the verbal press. "Do you know anything about this accident?"

"No, sir. I don't know anything."

"How about you, Danny? Do you know anything about this tragedy?"

"No, sir."

"And you, Sonny?" asked Mr. Fagan, pointing a crooked finger at me. "Do you know anything?"

"No, sir."

And so, Mr. Fagan went around the room, calling on each boy by name. But no one knew anything. Several of the boys outside our gang seemed a bit baffled by the vice principal's questioning, but they played dumb like the rest of us. I was sure that some of them had been through this kind of drill before. While Craig, Danny, and I sat up straight in our chairs and tried to look interested, the other boys slouched down low and avoided all eye contact.

"Well, boys, since none of you claim to know anything, here's what I'm going to do," announced our inquisitor. "I'm going to put all of you on detention for one week. That means that after the final bell rings for the day, you will report to me and sit in my office for one hour a day. During this time, you will do homework and think about whether or not you have anything to tell me about this accident."

So, the eight of us reported every day after school to Mr. Fagan's office. We sat there around the conference table and did our homework. And we said nothing. We didn't even talk amongst ourselves. We were all more than a little scared of mean Mr. Fagan. He had the power to kick us out of school and maybe even pack us off to jail.

As always, Craig was our guide. After that first meeting with the vice principal, he warned us in no uncertain terms. "Listen, guys. Do *not* say a word about anything to Mr. Fagan. He's just on a huge fishing expedition. He knows nothing about the accident and is just trying to sweat us until we talk. If we keep our traps shut, everything will be OK."

"But if we all stay quiet, can he suspend us from school?" I asked in a very weak and uncertain voice. I did not like the idea of detention and was positively paralyzed by the thought of suspension. What would my parents say?

"Of course he can't suspend us," harrumphed our leader. "Suspension is just for boys who do really bad things at school. So just stay quiet, and everything will be fine."

"But my brother says that Mr. Fagan suspended five boys last year," Danny objected. "And they weren't all that bad. They got framed by someone who told lies about them."

"Oh, shut up," said Craig, looking irritated by our ignorance. "Mr. Fagan can't suspend anyone unless he has some facts. And right now, no one has squealed on us, so he has no facts. And the three of us aren't going to give him anything to use against us."

I didn't know if Craig's advice was good or bad. All I knew was that I was too scared to even think about the accident. Since I couldn't even think about it, I knew that the last thing I would ever do was to blab to Mr. Fagan. What would I ever gain by spilling the beans to that sour old puss? He would just run off and tell the police, and then where would we be? All I wanted was for Mr. Fagan to disappear, and for the accident to fly on out of my life.

Since no one was talking, after our first week of detention Mr. Fagan gave us another week of reporting to his office. In this second week he turned up the heat. He summoned us one by one into his inner office. In these one-on-ones Mr. Fagan tried to distract us by his long stares, and confuse us by presenting more of what he'd learned. No doubt he'd been busy scurrying around the halls collecting information from other students. I know for a fact that he'd talked to our buddy Mike, who still knew nothing about the event. He'd also quizzed Tom, the quarterback of my football team at the park. But Tom also knew nothing.

"Sonny," he told me as soon as he'd closed the door, "you seem like a good boy who's probably just running around with the wrong crowd. So now might be the time to tell me the truth. Are you sure you don't know anything about this horrible train accident?"

"No, sir," I repeated. "I don't know anything."

"How about this boy named Todd?" continued Mr. Fagan, peering at me intently through his thick glasses. "Do you know him?"

"I've met him once or twice," I offered hesitantly, wondering how he'd even heard of Todd, "but he's not really a friend of mine."

"Do you happen to know if this Todd was involved in this accident?"

"No, sir," I answered, lying through my teeth. "I really don't know if he was involved or not."

"Did you happen to see this Todd on the day of the accident?"

"No, sir, I did not."

"Did you see or talk to him after the accident?"

"No, sir."

"But how can that be true?" exploded a suddenly exasperated Mr. Fagan. "I have a report lying here on my desk that claims that you and Craig and Todd were at the playground on the very afternoon of the accident."

"But that's not true," I replied as calmly as I could. "That report is wrong. I didn't see Todd on the day of the accident."

"Someone must be lying here!" shouted a clearly frustrated Mr. Fagan. "How can all of you boys know nothing? Can you please answer me that?"

"I don't know, sir."

"Well, some of you must know something!" cried Mr. Fagan. "And I'm going to get to the bottom of this by hook or by crook!"

The one-on-one interrogations continued throughout the week without Mr. Fagan learning anything new. As teenagers, we were all very good at playing stupid. We were especially good at playing dumb around authority figures like Mr. Fagan. The more he pressed, the less we knew about anything.

Also, it must be confessed, Craig, Danny, and I were learning how to lie—and lie well. At first, this bothered me a lot: everyone from my parents on up had taught me to tell the truth. But what else could I do? Todd and all my buddies were warning me *not* to tell the truth. And I was sure that they knew more than me.

I was always deathly afraid that my parents would somehow find out about these after-school detentions. I worried that either Mr. Fagan would call my parents or that they'd suspect something was up when I arrived home late from school day after day. Before the detentions had started, I'd always arrived home promptly at four. But when my mom asked one day why I was coming home so late, I invented a white lie about needing to stay after to catch up in algebra. Math was always my weakest subject in school, and my parents knew this. So, they never suspected the real reason why I was always coming home late. I lucked out, at least for the time being, but I was always worrying about when my luck would finally run out.

After these sessions with Mr. Fagan, walking home with Craig and Danny was usually a very sobering experience. We'd start out all quiet and depressed before Danny, the irrepressible one, would blurt out: "How much longer do you think we can go on like this? Don't you think there's someone out there who's eventually going to blab on us?"

"No, I don't think that anyone knows but us," Craig would reply quite matter-of-factly. "Unless one of us talks, we'll be OK."

"But how about if Todd talks?" I would venture. "He might be out of town, but he's certainly a big talker."

"No, that's not true," Craig would say, correcting me. "Todd's really not a big talker at all."

"How can you say that?" I would object. "Todd loves to brag."

"No, he doesn't," our leader would add. "Todd may brag around us, but he really hates the police. So, he won't say anything to the cops because he knows that he's the one who has the most to lose."

We'd walk on a bit before Craig would add, "Plus, Todd's done a lot of bad things in the past. Even if he did talk, I'd bet a hundred dollars that no one would believe him."

"But this is probably the worst thing he's ever done in his life."

"I'm not sure about that," Craig would say, correcting me again.

"Hell, look at it this way," Danny would interject. "If Todd ever talked, he'd have to take most of the blame for the event. It was his stupid idea—we were only doing what he told us to do."

"But how could you prove that it was his idea and not ours?" I would counter.

"Oh, everyone knows he's the one who does all the bad things around town," Danny would say.

"And then the worst they could say about us was that we were stupid," Craig would add. "Very stupid."

"But don't they send stupid people to jail?" I would ask.

"Yes, sometimes," Craig would reply. And then we would all grow quiet and pensive again.

I had the feeling that Craig felt the burden of these interrogations with Mr. Fagan more than the rest of us. After all, Craig was our leader, and he was the one who'd agreed that the three of us should follow the ne'er-do-well Todd. Without Craig, we never would have listened to anything Todd had to say. Looking at it this way, maybe Craig felt the most responsibility—after Todd, of course—for causing the accident. I don't know if this was altogether true, because I was never sure how much responsibility our leader felt for any of his actions. He seemed to act first and then let the chips fall as they might.

But once when we were walking home from school, Craig suddenly blurted out, "I don't know why I ever let that bad boy talk me into following him to the railroad station. I should've known he was up to no good."

"But Craig," I responded, "all three of us followed him to the station, and all three of us knew that he was a bad boy."

"Ah," said Craig. "You guys would've followed me to the end of the world. I should've put my foot down, and then none of this would've happened."

I couldn't think of any good reply.

Without a doubt, Craig could certainly lead us around by our noses. And maybe—just maybe—he could also feel responsibility for having this kind of power over us. Who knows? Craig didn't normally open up like this. Instead he was always trying to "lead from the front" by playing the tough guy who never had any second thoughts. He would pester and bully us to do new and ridiculous things, and we almost never questioned his intentions. For him, the process of meeting each new challenge seemed to be the most important thing.

I really don't know. It's hard to tell how anybody makes decisions, and I certainly didn't have a clue about how Craig's brain worked. Maybe he acted without thinking at all: the thrill of doing something new and different was all he needed. The only thing I can say for sure is that the three of us were feeling pretty miserable right about then, and we couldn't see much light at the end of the tunnel.

CHAPTER 9

With his left arm in a cast, Craig couldn't play any sports. So, on the weekends we didn't have much to do except hang around the playground. The organized summer baseball and other activities at the playground were now over, but many boys still came down to the place to play basketball. The playground had four or five outdoor courts that were always teeming with excitement on Saturday afternoons.

Craig couldn't play basketball because of his arm, and Mike and I couldn't play for lack of ability. I suspect that Danny, athlete that he was, could've joined the others out on the court. Danny could certainly dribble a basketball, and he also had a nice jump shot; I think he'd even played on a team when he was younger. But without Craig he was content to just sit with us up in the stands.

The four of us liked watching the older boys run around the court, passing and shooting. Some of the boys could really shoot and score. A few of the taller ones were always trying to dunk. None of them could do it, but it was fun watching their attempts to get above the rim.

One Saturday in October we were watching two well-matched teams go at it on the court when Danny suddenly piped up, "Hey, that's Grant, Todd's friend."

"Where?" asked Craig.

"That big guy standing on the other side of the court."

Grant was a large, powerful-looking boy with the beginnings of a brown mustache on his upper lip. He looked quite out of place on the sidelines. He was about five feet ten: a full head taller than anyone else around. I'm sure he could've easily dunked over anyone else on the court. On his way up to the rim, he probably would've mowed over a couple of the other players.

Grant must have spotted Danny about the same time that our friend spoke up, because he quickly moved over to where we were sitting. On his way over he yelled, "Well, if it isn't Danny Smith, Alan's kid brother. Hey, what are you up to?"

"We're just here watching basketball," answered Danny in a very wary tone.

"That's cool," Grant responded. "It's great to see you." Glancing around to see who else was in the stands, he added, "Say, I heard that you had a little trouble with Todd awhile back."

At the mention of Todd's name, Craig, Danny, and I froze in place. Ever since the accident we'd carefully avoided mentioning Todd's name in public. We rarely even talked about him among ourselves.

"Nah, we didn't have any trouble with Todd," Danny said, looking over to Craig for help. Craig had never met Grant before. Danny only knew him through his older brother.

"Aw, come on," Grant continued. "I'm not stupid. Todd told me the whole story. He said that you had a good time out on the railroad track."

Danny had no reply. Since Grant seemed anxious to continue the conversation, he pointed to the rest of us. "Are these your friends?"

"Yeah."

"Well, then, Todd's looking forward to seeing all of you when he gets back. He likes you guys."

Again, Danny had no answer. And Craig just sat there dumb, trying to decide what to do. I started wondering about when Todd, our nemesis, might return. And Mike—well, he looked just plain worried.

"Hey, guys," Grant rambled on, "why don't you climb down out of the stands so that we can talk? OK?"

Since he said this more as an order than a request, we quickly complied. Grant had short brown hair and a scar on his right cheek. He was tall and built like a brick—almost as considerable a physical presence as his friend Todd. Both of them had wide, strong shoulders and the kind of pumped-up arms that came from a lot of weight lifting at the gym. They also looked like they'd been in their share of fights. And both had that same odd, slightly out of place grin.

At this point Mike came to life and quietly excused himself. Mike was still in the dark about the accident; he didn't know anything about our role in the event. But he must have sensed that Grant was trouble, and so he decided that it was a good time to go home.

"Hey guys, relax," said Grant, trying to reassure us. "Don't worry, I'm not going to do anything to you. I just need your help."

"What kind of help?" asked Craig, suddenly perking up.

"I need you to walk with me over to the golf course."

Our town had a small, public golf course a couple of blocks from the playground. I'd never been there before. I didn't play golf and was pretty sure that none of my buddies did, either.

"To do what?"

"Don't worry. I'll show you once we get there."

"But why should we come with you," asked Craig, "if we don't know what you want us to do?"

Our leader was doing his best to try to push back against this hulk. He was also probably thinking back to the time that we'd followed Todd, without knowing what he was up to. Craig no doubt wanted to avoid a similar disaster.

"Let's just say that you're doing it for Todd," Grant said. "And if that's not good enough," he added in a more threatening tone, "I'll give you a couple more reasons."

With that our leader clammed up. It was a bright and beautiful fall day, and Craig probably figured that nothing bad could happen if we just followed Grant over to the golf course. After all, Craig knew nothing about Grant. And he probably figured it was best to let this big guy take over. In essence our leader adopted the same posture he did around Todd: he retreated into a watchful shell and waited for this new Napoleon to mess up.

As things turned out, this decision was unfortunate for all of us. As we soon learned, following Grant anywhere—even in broad daylight—was a mistake, a big mistake. It was a bit like following someone off a cliff.

At the golf course, Grant guided us over toward the clubhouse, which was a low-slung, one-story building with a wide outdoor patio overlooking the carefully manicured course. On this particular afternoon, the patio was filled with colorfully dressed middle-aged men, all nursing cool drinks after a hot day on the course. Some of them were reliving that day's exploits out on the course; others were simply lazing in the sun. None of them seemed to be paying any attention to their surroundings.

The golfers had all left their golf carts lined up at the back of the patio. The carts appeared abandoned and that's what attracted Grant's attention.

"Guys, here's what I need you to do," he said quietly as he ushered us around to the back of the patio. "I need for you guys to sit down on this brick divider and watch the patio while I mosey on around the golf carts."

"But why do we need to watch the patio?" asked Danny. "What are you going to do?"

"You guys just watch," answered Grant. "And let me know if you see anyone coming back here."

Craig glanced at Danny, and Danny looked at me. And we all got a sinking feeling that events were once again spiraling out of our control.

"And go *psst* if you see anyone coming," Grant added for good measure as he headed away.

"What happens if we do that?" Danny persisted.

But Grant didn't reply. He was too focused on the golf carts.

Hell, I thought to myself, *I bet he's going to steal clubs from these carts while we watch. And if he gets caught, the police will come and he'll get put in handcuffs, and we'll all get into a heap of trouble.*

Sure enough, that's exactly what Grant did. He moved slowly from cart to cart, lifting a club from one and two clubs from the next. He was quite indiscriminate in his stealing; he didn't take either the newest or the most expensive-looking clubs. He sauntered between the carts in a breezy, relaxed fashion; he certainly wasn't in any hurry. It all seemed like a game. How many clubs from how many carts could he make off with?

When Grant had seven or eight clubs in his hands, he began to stroll back to us. He continued walking very calmly, not at all anxious or worried. However, the three of us were beside ourselves with angst. Before Grant arrived, we all jumped off the wall and started fast pacing away from the clubhouse. Grant was a thief, and we were sure that someone was going to jump out of the shadows and nab him. We wanted to get as far away from Grant as we could before he got caught and hauled off by the cops.

I don't think that Grant ever ran or even fast-walked that day. Instead, he continued to stroll along, always working his way away from the clubhouse. All the time he moved, he kept mumbling to himself, like he was trying to decide which club to use on the next hole. The only problem was that he had all these clubs clenched tightly in his right hand and not neatly stowed away in a golf bag. So, I'm not sure how much he would have fooled any of the golfers out on the course. And he must have looked even more peculiar when he got off the golf course. I mean, who walks around the streets of a town holding a bunch of golf clubs in their hands? But Grant's tactics evidently worked, because no one ever stopped or challenged him.

Grant eventually pulled up to the rest of us at the playground. Smiling his lopsided grin, he chortled, "Now, wasn't that easy, guys?"

"No, it wasn't easy," responded our very agitated leader. "And it sure wasn't fun."

"Aw, lighten up. You guys are too uptight. That was as easy as taking candy from a baby."

"But what would've happened if you'd gotten caught?" Craig shouted.

"Oh, I never get caught. I've done that a million times," Grant said, clearly lying through his teeth.

"Do you always do it by yourself?" Craig pressed.

"Oh no. Usually I go with Todd. He's a pro at this. He's the one who taught me."

"That figures," snickered Danny.

One crook teaching another, I muttered sarcastically under my breath. *The two of you are the biggest crooks around here.*

"But what are you going to do with the clubs now?" asked Danny. "I'm sure you don't play golf."

"Oh, hell no. Golf is a stupid sport for rich people. I just sell the clubs to my friends."

"Do you have any friends who play golf?" I asked, really doubting whether Grant knew any golfers at all. He was the kind of guy who only knew other hoodlums. Like Todd.

"Of course I do," he replied. "And they'll pay good money for these clubs."

"How much?"

"Oh, fifty to a hundred dollars a club."

"A hundred dollars a club?" whistled Danny, making a funny face. "I'm sure no one would ever pay you that much."

But Grant did not answer.

Truth be told, I'm pretty sure that Grant really didn't know how much he could sell the clubs for. He probably gave them away to someone else to fence. Or maybe he just stored them in a garage somewhere, hoping against hope to sell them some day. Grant probably needed the money, but he seemed to be the type of crook who got as much enjoyment out of the act of stealing as anything else.

On that afternoon, Grant stowed his stolen clubs behind some trees at the playground. And then he tried to convince us to return with him to the golf course. "Why are you guys so afraid?" he sneered, smiling his weird half grin. "You've already seen how easy it is."

"But it's stealing," replied Danny. "And we don't want to get caught and hauled off to the police station."

"I'm telling you; I never get caught."

"But there's always a first time."

"Believe me—we won't get caught."

None of us would budge.

Seeing that he was getting nowhere with us, Grant tried adding in a sweetener. "If you go back with me this time, I'll pay you. When I sell the clubs, I'll give you half of whatever I make."

"But how do we know that you'll pay up?" asked Danny, who'd probably heard something about Grant's tactics from his brother.

"Believe me," replied Grant, putting on his best face. "When I talk about money, I always tell the truth. I promise that I'll split the money with you."

"But my brother says that you never pay up, even when you borrow money from other people," Danny yelled back.

"Ah, hell. What does your brother know? We never hang out together," replied an increasingly exasperated Grant.

"Come on, guys," he pleaded in a menacing kind of tone. "Do I need to tell Todd how you wouldn't help a friend? He wouldn't like that, I'm sure."

But threaten us as he would, Grant still couldn't get us to budge. No one would agree to go back with him.

In the end, Grant had to return to the golf course all by himself. None of us had ever served as lookouts for a crime before, and we certainly didn't want to repeat the experience. When Grant took off to steal some more, the three of us left the playground in a hurry. Grant could go recruit some other suckers to serve as lookouts; we wanted no more part of this sick petty thief.

CHAPTER 10

My new junior high was very different from my old one. Not only did it have Mr. Fagan, the strict disciplinarian, but it also had a lot more spirit. Maybe the principal and his staff thought that pep rallies were a good way of relieving all the pressure that we felt in the classroom. We certainly did a lot of homework every night, and during the day the competition among the kids in my classes was intense. I had to study more than ever before. Craig and Danny didn't seem to study as much, but they weren't in the fast-track classes. They were smart, but—unlike me—they had other interests. Both of them were much more into social events and activities.

I soon found myself really looking forward to our school's pep rallies. They took place at 10 AM every Friday morning before home football games. It was so much fun standing up, yelling as loud as you could, and forgetting about all your problems. The school band would play, the trumpets would blast, and the cymbals would sound out. And when they started beating on the drums, everyone would jump up on their wooden seats and begin chanting cheers for our junior high, Blair.

The pep rallies featured eight cute ninth-grade cheerleaders, the prettiest girls I'd ever seen. Of course, I didn't know any of these girls and I was too shy to even inquire about their names. It was as if they lived in another universe and came down from heaven only to lead us on at the pep rallies. But heck, I bet that even Craig was in the same boat; I really doubt if he knew all of their names. Craig was poised and confident, but I could tell that our woes and his broken arm were beginning to wear down even his natural assertiveness. So, when I would ask him about the cheerleaders, he would grow defensive: "Humph, of course I know them."

"But what are their names?" I would press.

"That's for me to know and for you to find out." And with that put-down, he would smile his all-knowing grin and quickly switch the topic of conversation. Craig was very good at bluffing when he was trying to hide what he didn't know. And I'm sure he didn't know as many ninth-grade girls as he claimed.

After a couple of pep rallies, Craig, Danny, and I became quite enamored with the shortest of the ninth-grade cheerleaders. Since we didn't know her name, we began calling her "the little cheerleader." She was always the quickest to smile and the one with the most energy. She would bound back and forth across the indoor stage doing cartwheels, handstands, and all kinds of gymnastic feats. And when it came time at the end for the cheerleaders to toss someone up in the air, she was always the chosen one. Launched high into the air, she would land perfectly poised, with head tossed back, shoulders straight, and the broadest of grins on her face.

Since we were only eighth graders, we never saw the cheerleaders in the halls or on the playground. This only added to their mystique and allure. Had we ever encountered one of them in real life, I honestly don't know what we would've done.

Now Craig, Danny, and I walked a mile to and from school every day. Our friend Mike—he with the overprotective mother who never let him have any fun—joined us on occasion, but usually it was just the three of us trudging back and forth to school. Our route took us along wide, tree-lined streets with very little traffic. To make things more interesting we cut in and out of a number of well-manicured backyards in order to check out what was happening at two small creeks in the area.

The creeks really fascinated us; we were always looking for signs of muskrat, beaver, and possum. Craig often talked about how we needed to set up traps in the creeks to see what we could catch, but we never followed through. Craig claimed that his father owned traps, but I'm pretty sure that he was bluffing us here too. I never saw any traps around his house, and our area was far too populated for anyone to do any animal trapping. Everyone knew that that was something only mountain men did out in the wilds of Montana or Alaska.

On our daily walks we rarely saw anyone from school. In the mornings we left too early to see any of our classmates. Since we meandered so much, we left at 7:00 a.m. sharp. In the afternoons our time in detention didn't help, because then we were walking home an hour later than everyone else. But maybe we just lived in the wrong direction from school. Many of our classmates lived much farther away and rode buses to school. From time to time we envied our friends who rode the bus, but in general we were pretty content walking to and from school.

One afternoon after detention something amazing happened: we spotted the little cheerleader walking just ahead of us on the sidewalk. Unfortunately, she was not alone. She was with Clark Foster, one of the stars of the ninth-grade football team. Of course, none of us knew Clark personally but we all recognized him from the school pep rallies. He was one of the players always singled out for special introduction by Mr. Brennan, the short, rotund coach of the ninth-grade team.

"And h-e-r-e's Clark, our star halfback!" Mr. Brennan would shout with a rolling flourish toward the end of every rally.

At the mention of his name, Clark would run up to the front of the stage, grin broadly, and bow solemnly to the left, center, and right before stretching his arms up in a victory sign. That was the signal for his football buddies to run up and join him on the stage. Locking arms, they'd all smile and bow to the crowd. With those theatrics complete, the drums in the band would start beating and everyone in the school would go wild, jumping up and shouting "Go Blair!"

On that afternoon after school, Clark and the little cheerleader weren't holding hands or anything. But they *were* animated and chatting easily. They obviously enjoyed each other's company, and the little cheerleader was smiling a lot. Clark looked like he was heading home after football practice, and the little cheerleader had probably stayed after school to meet him for the walk home.

"Hey, guys, this is our big chance," Craig said enthusiastically. "Let's follow them and see where the little cheerleader lives."

Craig was always up for challenges that presented themselves as easily as this one. And, unlike me, he was invariably curious about things that were probably a little bit out of his reach. He was always the fearless one; no obstacle was ever too great.

"Sure," replied Danny, eager as our leader to learn more about the little cheerleader. "Let's get closer so we don't lose them."

Since the street was wide and open, it seemed to me that we had little chance of losing them. We did, however, seem to have the chance of becoming too obvious if we moved too close. I didn't want to say anything, but I thought, *Wow, we're going to feel pretty stupid if they turn around and notice us.*

"She sure is short and tiny," observed Danny as we drew within talking distance of the couple. "She's about the same size as my little cousin."

"Hey, stupid," replied Craig, "that's the reason they throw her up into the air. She's the smallest cheerleader."

"And also the prettiest one," I added.

We did our best to follow them while still acting cool. However, we were only teenagers, and Craig's and Danny's voices were probably a little too loud. Clark, the football star who was at least a head taller and twenty pounds heavier than any of us, turned to flash us a clear but firm "Get lost" look. He didn't look at all pleased with us.

But we were all too smitten to take the hint. We did lower our voices and drop farther back. Or so it seemed to me.

"Quiet, guys," urged Craig. "Let's hush up so we can see what's happening."

Clark and the little cheerleader turned down one street and then up another. Although they were leading us off our usual track, we followed at what we thought was a fairly safe distance.

"Hey, guys!" cried Clark, suddenly wheeling around to confront us. "I told you to get lost. What's your problem?"

"We don't have any problem," replied Craig, always the unflappable one. "We're just walking home from school."

"Well, then, why are you following us?"

"We're not following you."

"Yes, you are!" yelled the by-now-agitated football star. "Every time we turn, you do the same. Why don't you take a different route? And do it *now!*"

"OK, OK," responded a suddenly chastised Craig.

Craig didn't like to be reprimanded, but we were certainly not in any position to argue. Clark wanted to be alone with his girlfriend, and he was clearly irked by our presence. And he was an imposing physical presence—someone not to be messed with. Maybe not quite as imposing as our hoodlum friend Todd, but he was up there. On the football field no one could bull over opposing players like Clark. And he actually seemed to enjoy running over other people. We certainly didn't want to be on the wrong end of Clark's anger. It seemed best for us to heed his advice and walk away from trouble.

Craig pointed out a detour for us to take that led through patches of woods and several backyards until we met up with our usual path home. The only problem was that after we'd reached our normal route, Clark and the little cheerleader appeared once again. This time they were holding hands and were much farther ahead.

"Hey, let's try to catch them again," Danny urged. "We're not doing anything wrong now because we really are on our way home."

"Are you sure we should do this?" I asked, thinking that this was really a dumb thing to do.

"Sure," answered our leader. "This time we'll just stay further back."

"But Clark seemed awfully mad last time," I said, trying my best to point out the obvious.

"Aw, you worry too much, Sonny. Don't be afraid. Everything will be fine if we just stay back."

So, Craig and Danny started to move closer to the couple, with me bringing up the rear. Despite my misgivings we steadily narrowed the distance. At some point Clark must have sensed something was up. Suddenly he wheeled around to confront us. But rather than shouting, this time he started to run at us. He obviously wanted to give us a good scare.

Craig and Danny bounded off into the woods. They were much faster than me and quickly disappeared through the trees. I did my best to follow them toward the creeks. Although I had a good head start over Clark, the football star was very quick for his size. So, he soon caught me stumbling through the undergrowth.

"You little bastard," he snarled, grabbing me by the shoulders. Whirling me around like a toothpick, he yelled, "I'm gonna teach you a lesson you won't forget!"

Clark smacked me in the face and punched me hard in the stomach. I crumpled to the ground holding my belly, and then he kicked me twice in the side for good measure.

"That should teach you!" he screamed. "And I'll do the same to your useless friends just as soon as I catch them." And with that he flew off after my buddies.

But Craig and Danny were too scared and too far away. Although Clark gave it his best, my friends managed to beat it through the woods. I was the only one that day to get pummeled. And I was the only one to learn how stupid it was to follow a football star and his girlfriend on their way home from school.

Since they never got caught, Craig and Danny learned nothing from this little misadventure. The next morning on our way to school Craig quite innocently asked me, "Did Clark ever catch you?"

"Yes, he did," I replied sheepishly. I didn't like to admit that I was too slow to run away from anybody.

"Well, did he do anything to you?"

"Nah," I replied, biting my cheek as I lied once again. "He only screamed and yelled when he caught me. And he warned us in no uncertain terms to stay away from him and his girlfriend."

"Hell," sniffed Craig. "Why do you think he got so sore? We didn't do anything bad."

"I bet the two of them are in love," piped in Danny. Like me, I don't think Danny knew the first thing about "love." But like any thirteen-year-old boy, he certainly enjoyed talking about it.

"You might be right," I offered. "Maybe we should leave them alone the next time we see them. After all, he's a lot bigger than us. And he did get awfully mad."

"Aw shit," objected Craig. "It's a free world. We should be able to walk behind them if we want."

Our leader could be pretty pig-headed about these things. Since he was so enamored with himself, Craig just assumed that everyone else loved him, too. This was definitely true for the three members of our little gang. We all admired and looked up to our leader. But this certainly wasn't true for others outside his sphere, especially for ninth-grade football stars. They clearly had their own set of followers and had no time for people like Craig. In fact, they probably didn't even know that people like Craig existed. I could understand all of this, but for some reason, Craig could not. He seemed to think that he was the sun to light up everyone's world.

I had the sinking feeling that someday this attitude would really get all of us into big trouble.

CHAPTER 11

Our town had a fenced-in park in the woods about a mile south of our houses. It was a dark and mysterious place: the trees and bushes inside were thick and overgrown, and there was never any sign of life within its borders. Bright red "No Trespassing" signs were posted at regular intervals on the high barbed-wire fence surrounding the park. Rumor had it that a large brick house sat on top of the hill in the middle of the place. However, the trees were so large and tall that no house (or any other structure, for that matter) was visible from the fence. Since no signs announced the contents of the park, it was anyone's guess what lay inside. Some boys claimed that the place was owned by a rich old lady who kept guard dogs on the loose around the grounds to protect her mansion. But we never saw any dogs running around. Others claimed that the park was owned by the Smithsonian Institution, which kept wild animals from Africa on the premises. But we never saw any wild animals, either.

"Do you know who owns this place?" asked Craig one fall Saturday afternoon as we strolled through the woods near the park.

"No. Who?" replied Mike, who had found a way to escape his mother's clutches and was now hanging around with us more.

When available, Mike was a nice addition to our gang because he was the quiet and agreeable sort. He was also smart in the sense of being a good and careful listener. Unlike most teenagers, he seemed to have a knack for remembering what different people had told him weeks or even months ago. When someone asked, he could recall all of those long-ago conversations in a flash. Mike could also remember the most mundane of everyday details. For example, he was always reminding me of the color of the shirt I was wearing on the day we'd first met. He was convinced that it was red, even though I could never remember owning a red shirt. Because of his prodigious memory, we used to kid Mike and call him "detective." We were convinced that someday he'd make a great police detective. But he didn't like that nickname very much and would always make a face when we used it.

Mike's main problem was that he was both timid and gullible. He was an only child, and probably his mother and father had always told him the truth. As a result, Mike was more than a little susceptible to the outlandish stories that Craig would dream up. While Mike would usually accept with a quiet shrug whatever Craig said, Danny would reject Craig's fantasies with a loud laugh or a sneer. Danny was always our leader's most vocal critic.

"The CIA owns the place," asserted Craig with a deadpan look of conviction that only he could muster. "And they use it to train secret agents."

"Bullshit!" cried Danny, who seemed sure this time that he could catch Craig in one of his dreamed-up fantasies. "That's nonsense. You've been watching too many spy movies, and you've started to believe all that junk."

"Yeah, well, do you want to bet on it?" replied Craig, always the one to wager money to try to bolster his preposterous ideas. The more ridiculous the notion, the more Craig was usually willing to bet. "I'll bet ten dollars that if one of us climbs over that fence and takes a peek around, he'll see one of those secret agents."

"I'll bet you on that!" yelled Danny, certain that he was going to win this time around. "I'm sure there are no secret agents in there. But how are we going to prove it one way or the other?"

Before the wheels in Craig's brain could spit out a reply, Danny answered his own question. "I know," he said. "Why don't we all climb the fence and see what's over there?"

"Well, I sure can't make it over the fence with this cast on my arm," Craig replied. "And I doubt if Sonny there can make it over, either."

I wasn't very happy being singled out here, but I could hardly object. I also didn't think that I could scale the fence. I *could* just picture myself getting stranded at the top by the two strands of barbed wire. Impaled up there, I'd hang suspended in midair until the buzzards came to pick me apart.

"Well, then, how about if I go over?" Danny suggested, still appearing to sense a great opportunity to win ten dollars.

"No, that wouldn't be fair," Craig objected. "You'll go over and claim that there's nothing over there in order to win our bet."

"No, I won't," fired Danny right back.

"Oh yes, you would!"

Craig always seemed a bit concerned about Danny's challenges to his authority. Danny, I think, never really wanted to take over our gang, but I do think he thoroughly enjoyed needling our leader and giving him a hard time. Danny liked stirring things up, and it was usually quite easy to get Craig going. A challenge here or a taunt there was usually enough to set Craig off: he was the excitable type, especially when he was trying to defend one of his harebrained ideas.

Craig seemed to consider the problem of the secret agents for a moment or two before announcing, "No, it's best if we send Mike over the fence. He's the lightest, and we can all help boost him over. And he always tells the truth."

"No! No way!" cried Mike in a loud and animated voice. "I'm not going over that fence."

In times like these, Mike usually had as much guts as I did. He was as honest as the day was long, but he was always the last one to join in any adventure. If the four of us ever had to line up to do anything, Mike would always be the last person in line. He would always be right behind me.

"Oh yes, you are!" said Craig, reaching out to reassure him. "If you climb the fence, I'll split the bet with you when you find the secret agents. How's that?"

"No," Mike yelled back, "I still won't climb that damn fence."

"Well, if you don't climb it," our leader replied quite evenly, "then you can't hang out with us anymore."

This was new territory: it was the first time I'd ever seen Craig give anyone an ultimatum like this. Usually he would wheedle and badger us in order to force his way. But in this instance, Craig probably figured that he just had to be tough. Mike was such a chicken that unless Craig stiffened him up, Mike would never do what he wanted.

Without a doubt, Craig's attempt to strong-arm Mike was influenced by the new and recent intrusion of the bad boys—Todd and Grant—in our lives. Craig had seen how they'd forced us to do things that we knew were wrong, and now he wanted to use the same tactics on Mike. Craig was learning new and evil ways, and he wanted to apply them to an easy target: our buddy Mike.

Poor Mike, I said to myself, *he's smart, but now Craig's going to force him to do something really stupid.*

Mike continued to insist that he wouldn't climb the fence, and so Craig had to spend several long minutes trying to whittle down his resolve. As always, Craig was determined and insistent, while Mike was wishy-washy and a bit unsure of himself. Mike clearly wanted no part of the fence, but he also seemed very anxious to stay in our gang. The three of us gave him something novel and interesting to do on the weekends, and I suspected that Mike probably didn't have many other friends. He was just too quiet and cautious to have a wide circle of buddies.

After carefully weighing his options and deciding that he couldn't very well run on home, Mike finally relented with a sigh, "OK, I give up. I'll climb the fence, but you guys have to stay right here watching me all the time. If I see anything spooky, I'm going to run back, and you have to get me over the fence as fast as possible."

"Agreed," replied Craig, flashing that famous "I won" smile. "We'll stay here right by the fence. But you have to promise to give a good look around in the woods before you head back."

So, we boosted Mike up and over the fence. It was a bit tricky getting him through the barbed wire, but he was small and lithe and with our help he eventually pushed through.

"Which way should I go?" he asked, just as soon as he'd dropped down on the other side of the fence.

"Head for the top of the hill!" ordered Craig. "That way you can see if there's a house up there. That's probably where the secret agents hang out."

"I'm telling you," snickered Danny, "you're totally nuts. He's not going to find any secret agents over there."

Mike disappeared into the dense, almost impenetrable undergrowth on the other side of the fence. Now that he'd been forced to undertake this mission, he seemed to be taking it seriously. He would either find the secret agents or die in the process.

Mike was gone for a good ten or fifteen minutes before we started to hear barking way off in the distance. The barking moved closer until we could hear the sound of someone thrashing and moving at great speed through the overgrown bush.

"Help, guys, help!" yelled Mike as he broke through the line of trees and headed for the fence. "Two huge dogs are chasing me!"

Sure enough, right behind Mike were two large German shepherds. Once Mike cleared the trees, the larger of the two dogs closed in on his heels. As our friend leaped for the fence, the lead dog lunged forward and bit Mike in the calf.

"Ow, shit!" he screamed at the top of his lungs. "That damn dog just bit me!"

Cussing at the top of his lungs, Mike scampered up the rest of the fence just as quickly as he could. Fortunately, he reached the top before either of the dogs could jump up again and bite him. Craig and Danny were waiting for him at the top and quickly pulled him through the barbed wire.

Mike was still yelling and hollering when he dropped to the ground on our side of the fence. He immediately yanked up his pant leg to show us the bite mark. It was all red and bruised, and the teeth marks of the enraged dog were clearly visible.

"Hell!" shouted Mike. "It hurts! It really hurts! Can't you do something?"

"Calm down, calm down," encouraged Craig as he bent down to examine the injured leg. "You're lucky; it doesn't look like the dog punctured the skin." Our leader was ever the optimist when it wasn't his leg that got bit. "I don't see any blood or anything."

"How can you say there's no blood?" hollered Mike. "It's all red, and it hurts like hell. And it's starting to bleed." He pressed on his left calf, and sure enough a small trickle of blood ran down his leg.

Anxious to calm Mike down, Danny sprang into action. He ran off and wet his shirt in one of the creeks. Returning he carefully wiped off Mike's calf and tore out a length of fabric from his own shirt. And then he carefully tied all of this around Mike's calf to stop the bleeding and make him feel better.

This really helped to quiet Mike down. He was one of those boys who didn't like the sight of blood, especially his own. For a time, I was worried that he might faint on us.

When Mike's cries had lessened to sobs, Craig—who, like me, had been doing absolutely nothing to help—suddenly perked up. "Well, what did you see over there? Did you see any secret agents?"

"No, I didn't see shit," hissed Mike, still very agitated and upset. "It was a big waste of time and energy."

"You mean you didn't see anything?"

"No! All I saw were weeds and bushes and trees. And then dogs, big dogs. And one of those goddamn dogs bit me."

"But were the dogs guarding a house or anything like that?" Craig pressed.

"Hell, there's no house. And the dogs weren't guarding anything. All of a sudden, they came tearing out of the woods. And then they were chasing me, and I got bit."

"Aw, calm down," urged our leader. "Since you didn't see any secret agents, we'll say that you and Danny won the bet."

This was a huge concession on his part. Craig was taking the extraordinary action of changing the terms of the bet against himself in order to quiet our friend down. I have to hand it to him; when the chips were down, Craig could really think quickly on his feet.

"But does that mean that Danny and I have to split the ten dollars?" Even though he was still sobbing, Mike was sharp enough to push for all he could get. This was his big chance, and he didn't want to blow it.

Craig paused a second before flashing a quick "Shut up" look toward Danny. And then he changed the terms of the bet even further. "No. Since you're the one who climbed the fence, you get to keep the whole ten dollars. You're the hero here."

Mike smiled a tight grin before Danny erupted, "Aw, shit, that's not fair! A bet is a bet, and it shouldn't be changed at the last minute. I was right all the time about there not being any secret agents. So, I should win everything."

"Oh, shut up," our leader yelled, glowering once again at Danny to stay quiet. "This is the best way to settle this."

"Still, it's not fair," said Danny, all worked up and clearly anxious to get the last word in. "At the very least I should win half the bet."

But our leader had spoken, and his decision was final. The concession to Mike clearly enraged Danny, but it was a smart one, I thought, because it made Mike feel a whole lot better. Mike was still whimpering and rubbing his left calf. And he was still complaining about what a stupid and "screwed up" adventure this had been.

"Look at this," he kept repeating. "I didn't want to climb that damn fence, and now I'm the only one who got bit."

However, once Craig stuffed the ten-dollar bill into his shirt pocket, Mike immediately perked up and started acting a whole lot more normal.

He quit sobbing and muttering obscenities under his breath. And after a couple more minutes, he quietly said, "Thanks for the ten dollars, Craig. And thanks for wrapping my leg, Danny."

And then right before he tried to stand up, with Craig supporting him on one side and Danny on the other, Mike added, "Boy, those huge dogs scared the hell out of me. I was sure they were going to tear me apart. I'm never going to do anything like that again."

CHAPTER 12

As I said, our junior high had a lot of school spirit. For our last home football game in November the school decided to put on a homecoming dance. Since we were eighth graders and soon-to-be top dogs at school, we felt more than a little pressure to find dates and attend homecoming.

But I had no inkling how to proceed. I'd never been on a date before, and I had no idea how to ask a girl out. Girls at our school were always giggling and traveling around in bunches. It seemed far too embarrassing to cut in on one of these groups, single out a girl, and then ask her out. *What would I say to her friends? And what clever thing would I say to her before popping the question: Do you want to go to homecoming with me?*

These things didn't faze Craig at all. He was always so poised that asking a girl out was no big deal. I think he was the first one in our class to get a date for homecoming.

"Hey, guys," he grinned one day on our way home from school. "Guess what I just did?"

"What did you do?" I replied, taking the bait.

"I asked Nancy to homecoming with me. And she said yes."

Nancy was the cute blond twin whom I'd met with Craig and my friends way back in June. Craig hadn't bothered to introduce me to her at the time, and I still hadn't mustered the courage to speak to her. She was always hanging around with the most popular girls at school, and to be perfectly honest I couldn't think of how to cut in and say anything to her. But I did notice that she half smiled at me whenever we passed in the halls.

"Why don't one of you guys ask Nancy's twin sister to the dance?" Craig rattled on with a grin. "Then we could double date."

Now, double dating seemed like an even more impossible challenge to me. Since none of us could drive, we'd have to ask our parents to transport us to the dance. That seemed totally embarrassing. *What would I say to my parents if they drove? And even worse, what would I say to my date in front of my parents?*

Danny and Mike must have felt the same way, because Danny quickly changed the topic of conversation. Danny could be outspoken around his male friends, but he was just as shy as I was around members of the opposite sex. He'd never had a girlfriend, and I was pretty sure that he'd never been out on a date. And Mike, well, he was just too quiet to be anything but hopeless around girls.

But Craig had planted the germ of an idea in my head. I started thinking, *If Craig can get a date, maybe I can, too.* So that night, I began plotting about how I might ask Susan to the dance. She was shorter and quieter than her more outgoing sister, which was just fine with me. If I was going to be tongue-tied around my date, it seemed OK if she was also going to be at a loss for words around me.

I had two weeks to act before homecoming. During those days I kept a close eye on Nancy and Susan at lunch and recess. I was looking for a time when Susan was away from her sister and all the other girls. Then I figured I could sneak up, make up some casual talk, and ask her to the dance. But

Susan always stuck close to everyone in her group, and I never spotted a good opening. So, my courage for acting out in the open quickly waned.

Instead, I decided to call her on the phone. Asking her over the phone seemed a whole lot easier than doing it in person. I wouldn't have to deal with all her friends. I also wouldn't have to look at her face to face when I asked. I was really worried about getting turned down, and I didn't know how I would handle that in public.

I got the twins' phone number from Craig and resolved to call Susan one night after dinner. Although we weren't in the same classes, I figured that I could begin by asking some innocuous question about homework. Then I could chat her up about some trivial matter before popping the question.

Two nights passed and then another. Finally, I summoned the courage to call on Thursday night, only eight days before homecoming. Since I'd never actually spoken to her before, Susan was quite surprised to hear from me. "Oh, Sonny," she answered. "You're one of the *last* people I'd ever expect to call me about homework."

"I'm sorry, Susan, but I wasn't paying attention when Mr. Kidd gave out the assignment in math class," I said, carefully following my memorized spiel. "I know that we're in different classes, but Mr. Kidd always gives out the same homework assignment to everyone. So, I thought that you could help me out."

"Oh sure, I'm happy to help," she replied, before giving me the details of a math assignment that I didn't need in the first place.

"Thanks, Susan. That's really helpful," I mumbled. I thought for a split second about something else to talk about, but naturally I drew a blank. I just wasn't any good at simple chit-chat. And when she didn't have anything new to add, the silence on the phone became oppressive. So, I quickly blurted out, "And say by the way, would you like to go to the home-coming dance with me?" Shy as I was, I just couldn't stay cool around a girl I hardly even knew.

"Oh sure, Sonny. I'd be happy to go with you." Susan was as gracious as I was stumbling.

And so, it was done. I had my first date.

On the night of the dance Craig and I double dated. Since I'd beaten him to the punch on Susan, Danny was unable to find a date. Danny might be able to talk a good line about girls among his buddies, but I think he knew about as many females as I did. And Mike never even mentioned members of the opposite sex, so he wasn't in the picture from the start.

Craig's mom offered to drive us both ways to the dance, which was fine with me. That way I wouldn't have to talk with my parents. At this point talking to my parents in social situations was almost as painful as chatting with a date.

On the way to the dance Craig and Nancy sat in the front discussing school. Craig always had a way with words, and his date seemed equally adept. The two of them flitted easily from topic to topic: from classes to teachers to homework.

Susan and I sat in the back of the car locked in an awkward silence.

"Do you like math?" I finally ventured, trying to break the ice.

"Not so much," she replied. "My favorite class is English."

"English, ugh." I moaned. "What do you like about English?"

"I like reading English novels, like *Wuthering Heights* and *Tess of the d'Urbervilles*."

Since I'd never heard of either of these books, I lapsed back into silence. Wracking my brain for something new to say, I eventually stumbled out, "And what kind of music do you like?"

"I like the Righteous Brothers."

Since I'd never heard of the Righteous Brothers, I added, "How about the Beach Boys? Do you like them?"

"No, not much."

And with that our conversation in the car ended.

The homecoming dance took place in our school's gym. It was decked out beautifully: with "Go Blair" banners on the walls, and blue and white crepe-paper coverings and placemats on all the tables. The tables surrounded a large dance floor set in the middle of the gym.

When we arrived, a loud rock band was playing Bobby Darin and Petula Clark tunes. A lot of people were either standing around listening to the band, but almost no one was out on the dance floor. We headed for one of the vacant tables in the far corner. On our way we spotted Tom, Craig's friend and the quarterback from our football game.

"Hey, Tom!" shouted Craig over the din. "Why don't you join us over here? There's plenty of room."

"Sure, that sounds fine," returned Tom. He was smiling as if he owned the world. And maybe he did, because he was holding hands with Holly, a real looker and one of the most outgoing girls in our eighth-grade class.

Athletes that they were, Craig and Tom immediately started talking sports, while Holly and Nancy, who were good friends, began discussing the latest hit records. In fits and starts Susan and I resumed talking about classes, until Craig abruptly announced, "Hey, folks, look at this." Grinning like a cat, he pulled a silver flask out of his coat pocket. "Guess what's in here?"

"I have no idea." Tom laughed.

"Well, it's bourbon that I stole from my parents' liquor cabinet. Does anyone want a sip?"

"Oh, Craig," said Nancy, instantly looking very ill-at-ease. "You're always trying to test the limits. What happens if you get caught?"

For weeks before the dance, Mr. Fagan and other school administrators had been warning us about no alcohol and no drugs at homecoming: anyone caught with these items would be immediately suspended from school.

"I don't know about this," I added, seconding Nancy's concern. "We'll probably get into big trouble if someone sees us." Indeed, several male teachers were prowling around the perimeter of the dance floor, keeping an eye out for trouble.

"Hell, I'm up for it," announced Tom, who was almost as much of a risk taker as Craig was. Tom would never be the one to sneak alcohol into homecoming, but hell, if someone else brought it, he would be the first to join in.

"Great," replied Craig, before looking over at the rest of us. "But what about you, girls? Do any of you want a sip?"

"No, I don't think so," Holly said with a frown. Since I thought she was the most likely of the girls to accept such a dare, her refusal should have alerted Craig. But it didn't.

"OK," replied our leader, looking only a bit disappointed. Gesturing toward Tom, he added, "How about if the two of us leave you all for a minute and go into the bathroom for a swig? Would that be all right?"

"OK, but don't get caught," cautioned Nancy, still looking very worried. "And please come back right away."

And so that's what they did. Craig and Tom made two successive trips to the bathroom, returning each time with slightly wider grins on their faces. Craig claimed they were very careful each time, locking themselves inside a single stall before taking a drink. But I had my doubts. Craig being Craig, the two of them probably opened the flask just as soon as they got inside the restroom. And then they probably asked other guys in the bathroom to join in the fun.

After the second trip to the bathroom, we started to dance. By now the anxious-sounding band had slowed down a bit and was playing music for couples to dance to. I liked dancing with Susan; she let me lead, and I could put my hand on her back. Craig and Tom seemed to dance almost cheek to cheek with their dates, but I was happy to maintain a more respectful distance. After all, this was my first date, and I wanted to be cautious.

Around this time our night began to fall apart. Back at our table, Craig insisted on making a third trip to the bathroom with Tom. They were gone a little longer this time. As they were leaving the bathroom, Mr. Fagan suddenly emerged out of the shadows. Tapping each of the boys on the shoulder, he said, "Gentlemen, can you please follow me outside into the hall?"

"Yes, sir," gulped Craig.

When they finally returned to our table, Craig and Tom were visibly shaken. Their faces were all white and strained, like they had just seen a ghost.

"Where have you guys been?" asked a very anxious Holly. "Did anything happen?"

"I think we're in big trouble," offered a suddenly contrite and humbled Craig. "Someone saw us taking sips from the flask in the restroom. So, Mr. Fagan caught us as we were leaving the bathroom."

"What did he say?"

"Mr. Fagan took the flask away," Craig continued, in a very weak voice, "and told us to leave the dance immediately. He also told us to report to his office first thing Monday morning."

"Oh no, that's terrible! Just terrible," moaned Holly, looking quite agitated and alarmed. "But we did try to warn you. I really hope that nothing bad happens to you on Monday."

Nancy, the more outspoken twin, was a whole lot blunter. On our way out she declared in a very firm voice, "Craig, we were all having such a good time until you did this. Next time you need to remember the people you came with. You have to remember that it's not all about you and what you want to do."

Craig looked up with an ashen face, but said nothing. And the usual grin on his face had turned into a tight grimace.

Craig and Tom suffered for their escapade big time. On Monday morning, Mr. Fagan gave each of them three weeks of detention after school. He also sent letters home to their parents describing in detail what they'd done. Craig's parents were furious when they learned of the incident. His father whipped him with a belt for stealing from his liquor cabinet, and his parents grounded him for a month of Saturdays.

I never heard what Tom's parents did, but I imagine he received similar punishment. While Tom was a carefree spirit, his parents were very strict. His father was a policeman in a different town. This was the first time Tom had gotten into trouble at school, so I'm sure that his parents came down hard.

While they suffered at home, both boys gained considerable notoriety for their deed at school. Among the boys, especially, Craig's standing climbed to new heights. He'd been the first to try to smuggle liquor into a school event and the first to ever get caught. Some boys were convinced that he was well on his way to becoming a "bad boy," while others were just jealous of his devil-may-care attitude toward life.

I personally didn't know what to think. On the one hand, Craig was my best friend, and it didn't seem right to bad-mouth him. To me he seemed like more of a daring free spirit than anything else. However, I did worry that his willingness to flaunt the rules might eventually get him into trouble. What would happen if one day he really did do something dumb and dangerous and got caught? Would the authorities then force him to confess to all his misdeeds going all the way back to the event at the railroad? Craig was certainly not one to spill the beans, I knew, but I was sure the authorities had their ways. And if he did talk, where would we be then?

CHAPTER 13

It was now mid-December, and Craig had been released from house arrest. We should have been happy that he was back to lead us around, but actually there was a growing sense of frustration among our gang. We were still very much strung out about the train wreck. It seemed like only a matter of time before Mr. Fagan or someone else would uncover our well-kept secret. Craig said that Mr. Fagan had pressed him to talk more about the event during his three weeks of detention but that he'd remained silent.

We were also feeling frustrated because it was the last month of the year. It was now too cold to play football in the park and too gloomy to wander about in the woods. And after our adventure in the fenced-in park, we had no desire to return to that place.

In short, we didn't have much to do on Saturdays. This was depressing, because Saturdays were our only day to escape from the pressures of school and homework. Saturdays were our designated fun days, when we could do something exciting.

So, we all perked up one Saturday morning when Craig announced, "Hey, guys, let's go holiday shopping this afternoon. Let's walk over to Preston and buy some presents for Christmas."

Preston was a nearby town with a wide variety of shops and stores. It had a long main drag where lots of kids hung out on the weekends. Many of these kids were drawn to a small but very popular record store located right on the main drag. This store was a magnet for teenagers because it stocked records from all the latest pop and rock groups. Some boys our age were getting interested in girls, but many more were busy following the latest records. Cool boys like Craig were trying to pursue both interests. Our leader was convinced that keeping up with the newest songs, and even better owning the most recently released forty-five rpm records, was the best way to stay popular with the girls.

Unfortunately, I was not at all excited by this shopping idea. I had no desire to become popular with the girls because they still scared and frightened me. Even more importantly, I had no money to go shopping. While Craig and Danny both received allowances and had extra money to spend, I had absolutely zero surplus funds. My parents steadfastly refused to give me a weekly allowance. They were always telling me how lucky I was, and how I should do my chores for free. I argued with them about this all the time but got nowhere. Without an allowance, buying records or almost anything else was totally out of the question.

As usual, though, I kept my feelings to myself. I couldn't tell my buddies that I was broke. They just wouldn't understand. At best they'd laugh at me. At worst they'd mock me and give me a new nickname—like "Cheapskate Sonny"—that would quickly spread all over the school.

Since no one objected to Craig's plan, within an hour the four of us started out for Preston. On the way Craig and Danny chattered about what they were going to buy. Mike and I kept quiet; I suspect that he had about as much spending money as me. I'd never seen Mike buy anything.

"I'm going to buy my mom a set of dish towels for Christmas," Danny bragged.

"Towels for Christmas?" Craig responded with a sneer. "That's stupid. I'm going to get my mom something much better than that. I'm going to buy her perfume."

Craig was nothing if he was not anxious to outdo everyone. I watched while Danny tried to think up a cutting reply. But this time he stayed silent. Sometimes it was just too much trouble to go toe-to-toe with our leader.

A couple of minutes later, in a round-about way to wrest control of our outing, Danny suggested: "Let's stop at the record store first. I want to get the latest Bobby Darin record."

Craig jumped on this idea. "Sure, let's stop there. I want to buy the latest Chubby Checker hit."

At Preston we headed straight for the record store. It was surrounded by a milling crowd of idle teenagers. I didn't pay these kids much attention; my circle of friends was limited, and I seldom recognized anyone I knew outside of school.

As we worked our way toward the entrance of the store, Danny said quietly, "Hey, there's Grant."

Now Grant was the last person any of us wanted to see. We had not seen nor heard from him since our experience on the golf course. And I knew that all of us—including Craig—wanted to keep it that way.

"Let's pretend like we didn't see him," whispered Craig under his breath. "Maybe we can make it into the store without him spotting us."

But Grant must have been on the outlook for people he knew, because right before we reached the door, he hollered out, "Hey, guys! Long time no see. How are you doing?"

"We're fine," replied Danny, turning around cautiously to greet him.

"Where are you going?" continued Grant, moving straight toward us.

"We're going to check out the new records," Danny offered.

"That's cool," said Grant. "It's good to see you. Todd sends his best. He's always asking about you guys."

At the mention of Todd's name, Craig, Danny, and I all seized up. Todd was our worst nightmare. It was bad enough running into Grant, but the specter of Todd being anywhere nearby was absolutely frightening.

Trying to seize control of the situation, Craig cautiously asked, "Have you seen Todd recently? What's he up to?"

"Yeah, I saw him about a month ago," replied Grant. "But he doesn't spend much time here. He's usually up with his dad."

Great, I thought. *I hope he stays there and never comes back.*

"Don't worry," Grant said, smiling his odd grin. "Todd will be sure to look you guys up when he returns. He likes hanging out with you."

And then, after a quick scan of the crowd, he added, "Hey, why don't you step over here out of the way of the door so that we can talk more privately? OK?"

Grant was an intimidating presence, so we promptly moved over. We had no desire to have this guy get mad at us in front of all these people. There was no telling what he might do. What would our friends say when they read in the papers, "Four Teenagers Beaten at Record Store in Preston"?

Right about this time Mike pulled his usual vanishing act and melted off into the crowd. We'd told Mike all about what Grant had made us do at the golf course, and he wanted no part of him. So, he decided to disappear on home.

"Hey, guys, don't worry," said Grant, in what was for him a reassuring voice. "You always seem a bit worried around me."

"Nah, we're not worried," Craig replied, trying his best to act cool. "We just want to get into the store."

"Well, don't worry," Grant rattled on. "I'm not going to make you do anything bad. I'm just going to ask you a small favor."

"What's the favor?" asked Craig, most likely thinking back to the last time this guy had asked us to do something for him.

"Ah, it's nothing, really," Grant purred. "I just want you guys to get me the latest two Beatles records from the shop. I don't have any money, and I'm sure you guys would like to help out an old friend."

Old friend? Bah! I thought to myself. *We've only seen you once before in our lives, and that time you made us help you steal golf clubs. You're just a tough guy who's trying to force us to do something bad again.*

Craig must have had the same thought, because he visibly blanched before saying, "Why would we want to do that?"

"Well," said Grant in a more sinister tone, "let's just say that you want to do it for Todd."

"But we hardly know Todd," protested Craig.

"That's not true," Grant shot right back. "Todd likes you guys. And if you don't want to help Todd, well then, I can talk to some people."

"Who can you talk to?" said Craig, being a bit more forward than he probably intended. Our leader was just trying to avoid being bullied, I knew, and he wasn't getting any help from either Danny or me. Both of us had gone mute.

"Let's just say that they're people you don't want to know."

Craig glanced over at the two of us. But we still offered no support. Unsure of exactly what to do, he thought for a long moment before replying in a strained voice, "OK, we'll do what you want. But you have to stay out of the store and wait for us here."

Craig must have sized up the situation and decided that we didn't have any choice in the matter. Grant was big and mean enough to get what he wanted. And if he didn't get it out of us here, then he would probably get it out of us later.

However, our leader clearly didn't want Grant to follow us into the store. There was no telling what this unpredictable hoodlum would have us do inside. Looming over our shoulders, he'd probably tell us to steal a record from every section of the store.

"Fine, I'll wait for you out here," Grant said, smiling broadly. "But don't be long, and don't come back empty-handed." He seemed pleased—but not at all surprised—that he'd forced his way on us. He was a cocky tough guy: one who always seemed to get what he wanted from those he picked on.

"Hell, now what are we going to do?" cried Danny, just as soon as we'd pulled away from Grant. "I certainly don't have enough money to buy Christmas presents *and* get these two Beatles records."

"Neither do I," said Craig with a grimace. Lowering his head, Craig thought for a second or two before sighing deeply. "Here's what we're going to do," he announced in a pained voice. "I'll go over to the section with the Beatles records and try to chat up the sales clerk. While I'm doing that, you guys are going to take the records and put them under your coats. Then we'll head for the door one by one. OK?"

"Do we have to do this?" asked Danny in a hushed tone. "This doesn't seem at all right to me."

No, this isn't right! I screamed to myself. *This is an insane idea. I've never stolen anything in my life! What will my parents say if I ever get caught?*

But I didn't have the courage to speak up. I just looked up at Craig to see what he would decide.

"Yeah, I think we got to do it," our leader said at last. "We don't have any choice."

"Can't we just run?" Danny suggested.

"No. There are too many people around and no place for us to run to."

"But each of us could run a different way," Danny pointed out.

"No, that wouldn't work," replied Craig, looking dejected. "Sonny's slow, and I still have my cast. So, he would probably catch at least two of us. And then he would just make the two of us do his dirty work. We just don't have any choice."

Silently the three of us entered the store and headed toward the section with the Beatles records. Danny and I began to idly leaf through the records, while Craig angled up to the young female clerk. Craig had a way with girls, and soon he and the sales clerk were chatting away. I have to hand it to our leader: one minute he was being threatened by Grant and the next moment he was amiably shooting the breeze with this girl.

With the attention of the sales clerk diverted, Danny and I went to work. Out of the corner of my eye I watched Danny snatch one of the Beatles records and stuff it under his coat. He then resumed leafing through the records like nothing had happened. A few minutes later, with my heart pounding like a drum, I did the same. But I couldn't go on thumbing through the collection after I'd taken the record; my hands were simply shaking too much.

Craig and the sales girl were laughing as Danny headed for the door. I waited until he was safely outside before I made my exit. I was sure that everyone in the store had seen me snatch the record. And I was sure that all the bells would sound when I passed through the door. But no one tried to stop me when I left, and no alarms went off.

Once we were safely outside, the two of us waited for Craig to arrive. We definitely wanted him to give the stolen records to Grant. Danny and I were through with this thug; we had no desire to deal with him anymore. Craig was the one who'd agreed to get the records, and so he should be the one to hand them over to this bum.

Where will this ever end? I thought, as I watched Craig hand the stolen records over to Grant. *This bad boy is just going to make us do horrible things every time he sees us.*

"Here's what you wanted," our leader practically hissed. "Now just go and leave us alone."

"Thanks a lot, guys." Grant snickered loudly. "I'll be sure to tell Todd that you say hi. He's always asking about you guys."

On our way home from Preston that day, I began wondering why Grant had singled us out for such treatment. *Did Todd tell him that we were a bunch of easy-mark suckers? Did Todd say that with a little "persuasion" we'd do anything? Or did Grant just get his kicks out of pushing younger kids around?*

In the end I kind of decided that Grant was just an incorrigible bully who liked to torment anyone he could. He was exactly like Todd: a mean boy who used the threat of physical violence to get whatever he wanted.

I decided that in the future I just *had* to stay away from both of them. And from that damn record store. In my mind, Grant, Todd, and that record store were all linked together. They were all bad news. And I think Craig probably felt the same way, because he never again suggested that we go to the record store in Preston.

CHAPTER 14

About this time, I started having nightmares about Todd and Grant. Danny said that he did, too. But I don't know about Craig. Every time I asked him, he would try to change the topic. Craig was like that: he would never confess to any kind of weakness. Around us he tried to maintain the same upbeat and cocky manner. But I bet that he had the same frightening dreams that the rest of us did.

My nightmares were usually of the same variety. I'd be walking in the woods by the train tracks on a bright fall day with Craig and Danny. All of a sudden a policeman—someone who looked a lot like Mr. Fagan but bigger and meaner—would jump out of the woods shouting, "Hey! Where are you kids going? You're supposed to be down at the police station in half an hour."

The three of us would look at each another blankly, shake our heads, and turn around and head for the station. Somehow along the way, Danny would always manage to slip away into the woods. And so, when we arrived it would only be me and Craig who had to face the music.

At the station "Mr. Fagan" would usher us into a large interview room, complete with one-way mirrors running along the whole length of one wall. At the single conference table inside the room, our two mothers would be sitting bolt upright in straight wooden chairs. Each of them looked pained and exasperated.

Inside the room the questions would come flying in waves, just like in the movies. "Where were you on the afternoon of August ninth?" boomed the Mr. Fagan look-alike.

"We were at the playground," replied Craig, speaking as always for the both of us.

"And who were you with?"

"We were there with our buddies, playing baseball."

"No, you weren't!" yelled Todd, suddenly materializing out of nowhere and leering at us with his lopsided smile. "You were with me down at the railroad tracks."

"No, I swear," Craig protested. "We were playing baseball at the playground that day!"

"Liar!" cried Todd.

"Oh, why do you lie to us, son?" Craig's mom shouted, trying to drown out Todd's insistent tall tales.

"I'm not lying, Mom. I'm telling the truth."

"And how about you, Sonny?" yelled the Mr. Fagan look-alike, abruptly turning his attention on me.

"I was with Craig, and the two of us were at the playground, just like he said."

"And what were you doing there?"

"Playing baseball, just like Craig said."

"Oh, Sonny," my mom moaned, with the most sorrowful look on her face. "How can you lie to us about something like this? You've always been such a good boy."

RICHARD H. ADAMS, JR.

"Aw, he's never been a good boy," interjected Grant, who'd suddenly appeared, like his buddy Todd, out of the blue. "Just tell them what you did at the record store."

"What record store?" shouted "Mr. Fagan," arching his bushy eyebrows in apparent confusion.

"The record store where he stole the records!" Grant cried.

"Oh, Sonny," wailed my very distraught mother, "how could you ever steal something? We didn't raise you like that."

"He's become a bad boy!" Grant yelled. "A real bad boy."

"No, I haven't."

"Do you want me to tell more?" hollered Grant, smiling wildly at each of us gathered around the table.

At this point I'd always wake up from my nightmare. My ears would be ringing and my head throbbing. And I'd feel very sad and like I didn't have a friend in the world.

One cold morning in January I must have been looking particularly overwhelmed, because my history teacher, Mr. Donald, asked me to stay after class. Mr. Donald, a young, energetic thirty-year-old, was my favorite teacher. His lectures on American history were colorful and inspiring, and he seemed to be genuinely interested in his students. He would joke around with us in class and slap us on the back in the halls. He seemed especially drawn to the shy and studious types, like me. He tried his best to draw us out of our shells.

"Sonny, what's up?" he said to me on that cold January morning. "You didn't do very well in our last test."

"I'm sorry, Mr. Donald. You're right: I flubbed that test. I guess I didn't study hard enough."

"You're right about that, Sonny. That was the lowest score you've ever had on one of my exams. What's wrong?"

I couldn't think of a good reply, so I waited for Mr. Donald to continue. I could tell by the concerned look in his eyes that he had more to say.

"But that's not all, Sonny. Lately you always seem so distracted in class. Whenever I look at you, your mind seems to be a million miles away. What's up?"

"I don't know, Mr. Donald," I replied rather sheepishly. "I really don't. I guess that sometimes I feel kind of depressed."

"Depressed? How can you feel depressed?" Mr. Donald sniffed. "You're young and smart and have your whole future in front of you."

"Oh, I don't know about that. The future is so far away. And right now, I feel like I have a boatload of problems on my hands. And I don't know what to do."

"What kind of problems?"

"Oh, I don't know," I replied hesitantly. "Problems of growing up, I guess."

"Girl problems?"

"No, I don't have any of those."

"Well, I'm sure that whatever problems you have," continued my teacher, "they aren't that great. You just need to buckle up and face them one at a time. That will make them disappear."

"Thanks, Mr. Donald," I answered skeptically. "I'll start working harder and paying more attention in class."

"Good," replied my teacher as I started to walk away. "And if you ever need someone to talk to, you can always come see me. I'd be glad to help."

"Thanks, Mr. Donald."

But the very last thing I wanted to do was to talk to anyone about my troubles, so my spirits remained just as gloomy as the outside weather. I moped around from place to place waiting for the next weekend to arrive.

One Saturday at the end of January, Craig decided that he just had to do something to raise our spirits. So, on the day after a huge ten-inch snowfall, he announced another one of his brainstorms. "Hey, guys," he declared with all the go-to enthusiasm of a five-year-old seeing snow for the first time. "Today we're going to play 'whipple pull' out in the woods."

"What the hell's 'whipple pull'?" Danny snorted.

"It's a new game I just invented," smiled our leader. "I have a big log down in the basement. We're going to hammer a bunch of nails into it and call it a 'whipple.' And then I'm going to pull the whipple with a rope through the woods, and you guys are going to try to follow me."

"You mean we have to track you like Indians?" asked Danny skeptically.

"Yep. You have to give me a fifteen-minute head start, though. And the rules say that I have to always pull it through the snow so that you can follow me. I'm only allowed to pick up and carry the whipple across streams and roads."

"Where do these rules about this new game come from?" I asked doubtfully.

Craig grinned broadly. "From my head. Where else do you think they'd come from?"

So, we went downstairs and hammered the nails into the whipple, and Craig pulled it out into the woods. We gave him the required head start, and then the three of us—Mike had joined us that day—bolted after him.

The sky was gray and overcast after the storm, so the light on the snow was pretty flat. Still, at first it was great fun bounding through the light, new-fallen snow. Even with ten inches on the ground it was not difficult running through the white stuff. It was also easy for us to follow Craig, because the whipple made a clear and broad track in the snow.

But after a while Craig must have decided that things were too easy and that we needed more of a challenge. So, about twenty minutes into the game, the tracks of the whipple would suddenly stop, before reappearing without warning twenty or more yards away. Craig was obviously revising the rules by picking up and carrying the whipple to throw us off track.

After another twenty minutes, he changed the rules yet again. This time he was a lot more devious. He began crossing and recrossing the small, half-frozen streams in the area. Each time he did this, he would carry the whipple a good ways beyond the stream. This made it much more difficult for us to follow him. It was also more of a pain in the neck because each time we crossed one of these streams our feet got all wet.

"This sucks!" exclaimed Danny as we splashed through the frigid water for the third or fourth time. "How about if we try to end this damn game by just catching up to Craig?"

"And how do we do that?" I asked.

"Craig is just going back and forth across these streams. So, if the three of us split up and fan out, we should be able to catch him."

"But how about if we get lost?" I objected.

"Aw, don't worry," Danny assured us. "We know these woods like the back of our hands. And how could you ever get lost so close to home?"

I wasn't convinced. With my terrible sense of direction, I knew that I could get lost by just going around the block. All the trees in the woods looked exactly the same to me, and the ten inches of snow on the ground made it impossible to make out any familiar landmarks. I thought that if we split up, I'd wind up walking to Siberia—all by myself.

Mike, as usual, said nothing against Danny's new plan. He seemed to have a better sense of direction than me, and he was definitely more adept at following the tracks in the snow. Mike was not very adventurous, but when focused on a task he could usually do it.

And so—just like Danny ordered—the three of us fanned out in the woods. I started walking and then running on the far-right flank. Pretty soon I lost sight of my two buddies. Even more worrisome was that I could no longer spot any of the whipple tracks in the snow. So, I slowed down and started looking all around in the woods every twenty yards or so. Maybe I should have hollered out to my friends, but I didn't want to seem scared. I was sure that someone or something would appear at any moment.

Eventually I reached the embankment for the railroad. I couldn't remember if Craig had given us any instructions about the railroad. *Is this one of the boundaries for the game?* I wondered. *Is Craig allowed to carry the whipple over the railroad tracks?*

I didn't know what to do, so I climbed up the embankment to see if I could see anything. Nothing. No sign of Craig, the whipple, or my fellow trackers. The woods were as empty as on the day they were created. I began thinking that I'd already arrived in Siberia.

Putting on a brave face, I clambered down the embankment, and continued walking in the woods. Pretty soon the trees opened up and the ground became flat and mushy. And then the earth became downright swampy, with a thin layer of ice covering everything. Walking on this crusted ice was difficult, because I kept slipping and falling through. My feet grew wetter and colder with every step.

Finally, I came to a back road that I'd never seen before. By now I was convinced that I was hopelessly lost. I was also pretty sure that going back the way I came would only lead to disaster. So, I decided to start walking along the half-plowed road, hoping for the best. Maybe I could flag down a car to give me a ride back into town.

With wet and frozen feet, I walked and walked, but no car passed by. Maybe no one was venturing out after the storm. Or maybe no one ever used this deserted back road in the first place.

I walked until it got dark. And then I became very worried. Finally, well after sunset, I reached a lonely gas station by the side of the road. The station was closed for the night, but it did have a phone booth. Luckily, I had a few coins in my pocket and was able to call home.

"Sonny, where are you?" wailed my mother, just as soon as she heard my voice. "It's been dark for almost an hour, and you're still not home!"

"Mom, I'm sorry, but I've been out hiking in the woods. And now I'm lost and have no idea where I am."

I did my best to describe my location: "I'm at a deserted gas station on a back road somewhere near the railroad tracks…No, I don't know the name of the road I'm on…No, I really don't even know what direction I am from home." Finally, I begged, "Can't you please come and get me as soon as possible? I've walked for hours, and my feet are like frozen blocks of ice."

It took my parents a good two hours to find me. After calling Craig's mom, my mom was able to get a rough idea of where Craig and the boys had last seen me. But they couldn't tell her exactly what direction I'd headed after we split up, so it took my parents a long time to locate the back road where I was stranded.

During the whole time that I waited, I stayed in the phone booth trying to stay warm by blowing on my hands and jumping in place. The flimsy booth offered the only protection against the steady wind and the falling nighttime temperatures.

When they finally arrived, my mom hugged me and my dad smacked me on the side of the head "for being dumb" and for getting lost in the woods. And then he brought out his belt and whacked me on the rear end five or six times "for good measure." Since my bottom was frozen—but not quite frozen enough to be numb—his switches really hurt.

On the way home, my parents hollered at me some more for getting lost in the woods. And they solemnly announced that I was grounded for the next four weeks. But by that point I didn't care at all—I was just happy to be warm and headed home.

CHAPTER 15

In mid-February something wonderful and totally unexpected happened: I got invited to the twins' Valentine's Day birthday party. These were the same twins—Nancy and Susan—whom Craig and I had taken to the homecoming dance. Since I hadn't said a word to either of them since homecoming, I'm sure that the invitation came through Craig and didn't have anything to do with me. I was just lucky enough to be Craig's friend, and as such considered important enough to invite.

Although it was dubbed a Valentine's Day birthday party, it was actually being held on the last Saturday in February. This date was supposedly closer to the twins' real birthday. But according to Craig, who always seemed to know everything about such things, the true reason was that the twins' parents had agreed to be out of the house that day. They'd help plan and set up the party but then would leave during the actual event.

This all sounded very risqué to me; my parents would never have done something like that. But when I raised this with Craig, he urged caution: "Yeah, it sounds like it might be exciting. But the twins are pretty conservative, so you never know what might happen."

"Do you know who else is coming?" I asked, anxious to gather as much information as I could about the event.

"Yeah, I think that Tom and Holly are coming." They were the couple who'd attended homecoming together. "And I think that Holly's younger sister will also be there."

"Anyone else?" I was sure that he was holding out on me.

"No, that's all I know so far."

The birthday party was an afternoon affair, from two to five, which perhaps explains why the twins' parents had agreed to be gone. Certainly, being absent for an afternoon party was very different from being gone for an evening one.

Craig and I arrived a bit late. Nancy, the more outgoing of the twins, greeted us warmly at the door. "Craig and Sonny, it's really nice to see you," she beamed, looping her arm through Craig's right arm. "The party's downstairs, so let's head on down there."

Eight or nine kids were already in the basement, which had paneled walls and a shiny hardwood floor. The kids had grouped themselves by gender. Tom and the boys were standing along the far wall, where the cake and tableful of snacks were set out. The boys were nervously fingering cans of soda and doing their best to make small talk. Holly and the girls were all laughing easily by the stairs, giggling at something Holly's younger sister, Coleen, had just said. Coleen, a dark-haired and precocious seventh grader, was almost as good-looking as her sister.

Craig stopped to greet the girls, while I headed over to the boys. Except for Tom, I really didn't recognize any of the other guys. One of them, Patrick, a tall, redheaded Irish American, looked vaguely familiar to me from school, but the other two did not. I decided that they must go to Catholic school. The twins were good Catholics, so even though they attended public school, they had a lot of friends at the local parochial school.

"OK, everyone!" proclaimed Nancy, the self-appointed head of festivities. "We're going to start off by doing the limbo. You all know how to do this: you go under the stick as low as you can with your back bent over to the floor. 'How low can you go?'" she added, snickering loudly while trying to mimic the low baritone voice of Chubby Checker, who'd popularized the dance. It was all the rage among teenagers.

Nancy put Checker's "Limbo Rock" on the record player, and we gathered in front of the limbo stick. Naturally, Craig and Tom were the first to try slithering under the stick. They succeeded easily because the stick, at first, was set at a reasonable height off the ground. Encouraged by their success, Holly and the hostess, Nancy, also maneuvered their bodies this way and that in order to pass under. By this time everyone was laughing and talking loudly. So, Susan, the other twin, and Coleen also gave it a shot. After some strange bodily gyrations, they also succeeded.

"Go ahead, Sonny!" Craig yelled, anxious to get the rest of us wallflowers involved. "I'm sure you can make it."

After Patrick went, I tried. Much to my surprise, I also passed under the stick.

Once they started lowering the stick, however, people quickly began dropping out. First, Susan and Coleen knocked down the stick and were eliminated, and then Patrick hit the stick and was tossed out. On my turn I struck the stick with my chest going down, and everyone hooted and hollered at my lack of coordination.

By the time the stick was set at its lowest point, only three people—Craig, Nancy, and Holly—were left in the game. Craig did his best to slither as low as he could, but he was no match for the lithe and supple girls. Holly eventually got the lowest and won the contest.

Just as we were finishing the limbo, we heard a loud, insistent rapping on the upstairs door. "Are we expecting anyone else?" Nancy asked, turning toward her sister with arched eyebrows.

"No, I don't think so," Susan replied smoothly. "I'll go see who it is, and you continue on directing things down here."

Susan was gone for a minute or two before we heard loud shouting: "No! No! You can't come in. Get out!"

"But I just came by to see Coleen," a deep—but not unfamiliar—male voice urged back.

"She told me to come over."

Sensing trouble, Craig jumped up and started bounding up the stairs, two at a time. Before he was halfway to the top, however, who should appear on the landing but Grant! None of us had seen (or heard of) him since our unpleasant experience with him at the record store. And none of us had any idea that he knew any of the girls here. Especially not Coleen, a mere seventh grader. Grant, big bully that he was, seemed focused on tormenting and pushing smaller boys around. As far as we knew, he had no interest in girls.

"Grant," exclaimed our leader, "what are you doing here? Did anyone invite you?"

"No, no they didn't," shouted Nancy, rushing up the stairs trying to restore order.

"You're going to have to leave right now!"

"Hold on, hold on," Grant said, lowering his voice and stretching out his hands in almost a pleading manner. "Coleen here said that it'd be OK if I stopped by. Didn't you say that, Coleen?"

At the second mention of her name, Coleen looked around apprehensively, seemingly stunned. But being of a strong-willed nature, she quickly recovered. "No, I never said anything like that. I think I told you that I was going to a party, but I never said that you were invited."

"Hold on," cried out Holly, her older sister. "Where in the world did you ever tell him something like that? I've never seen this guy before in my life."

"Don't you remember bumping into him last Saturday at the record store in Preston?" Coleen replied evenly. "That's probably where I told him about the party."

"And why would you do that?" pressed Holly, suddenly looking quite irritated with her sibling.

"Because I wanted to."

"Relax, relax," cried Nancy, separating the two sisters with her hands and trying again to gain control of the situation. "No more squabbling among sisters. And you, mister," she said, stiffening her voice and pointing a sharp finger at Grant, "you just have to leave. Right now!"

"And what if I don't?" shot Grant right back. He was not the type of guy who liked being bossed around by anyone, especially by a girl.

"I'll call the police," Nancy hollered.

At the mention of the police, Grant immediately tensed up. His face reddened, and his fists tightened up. He looked mad, like he wanted to haul off and hit someone. The only question was whom? He couldn't very well hit Nancy, because she was of the wrong gender. Even a bum like Grant wouldn't hit a girl—I think. And Craig, and all the other boys, were, for the moment, out of his range.

"Whoa, whoa, wait a minute!" intervened Craig, ignoring the very angry look on Grant's face. "Let's not come to blows here. Let's try to settle this thing peacefully without the cops."

With these words, Grant relaxed a bit. Our leader moved up the stairs toward Grant while continuing to talk. Craig was great at improvising on the fly in situations like this.

"Grant," he suggested, "how about if you take a soda here and then go outside with Coleen and talk things over? Would that be OK?"

Grant shot a mean look at our hostess while considering his options. There were ten of us in the basement, and no one seemed to welcome his intrusion. Even Coleen, the object of his attention, didn't appear at all pleased. Grant was certainly used to forcing his will in tight spots, but this time the odds seemed stacked against him. So, he replied in a very grudging voice: "I guess that'd be OK with me. How about you, Coleen…would that be OK? I really need to talk to you."

"Sure, that'd be fine," said Coleen, who now seemed quite anxious to end this strange home invasion.

Smiling his famous "I won" smile, Craig ran down the stairs, got Grant a soda, and handed it to him with a friendly clap on the shoulder. I'm sure that Craig still didn't much care for Grant, but he clearly relished his new-found role as peacekeeper. Craig was, after all, a showboat and was keen on anything he could do to show off around the girls.

Grant and Coleen left the party, and we never did see Coleen again that afternoon. Only at school the next week did we hear that the two of them went into town for a soda. Coleen was really a free spirit who seemed to do exactly what she pleased.

"Just wait until I get home tonight and tell my parents what happened," crowed Holly, her ever-watchful sister who was anxious to rein her in. "Coleen is gonna get grounded for a month!"

Grant's sudden appearance—and departure—put a real damper on the festivities.

Nancy, our hostess, struggled to get us back into a party mode. First, she tried to get each of us to stand up and belt out our best version of the Beatles' "I Want to Hold Your Hand." That failed when all of the boys—including Craig—refused to sing. Next, she announced a contest where we were supposed to get up and dance our best rendition of Chubby Checker's "The Twist." That effort ended when only two couples—Craig and Nancy, and Tom and Holly—got up and danced. The rest of us were either too shy or inhibited to show off our "twisting skills" in public.

Not knowing quite what else to do, Nancy finally suggested, "How about if we play an old favorite: spin the bottle?"

"Oh hell!" yelled Tom sarcastically. "That's an old grammar school game. We're too old for that."

"Yeah, that's a stupid game!" shouted someone else.

"Oh yes, we can play that game, and we're going to play it right now," a suddenly determined Nancy answered right back. "This is a great game to get things going again. It's also a good game for couples and couples-to-be."

Now I have no idea who Nancy was referring to when she said "couples-to-be," since there were surely only two couples in the room: Craig and Nancy, and Tom and Holly. As far as I knew, there were no couples-to-be at the party. But I certainly didn't know everything.

Right after Nancy said this, she shot a meaningful glance at her sister. And then Susan turned and gave me an encouraging grin. It seemed like the twins were scheming and plotting behind my back!

We sat down in a circle and our hostess spun the bottle. It landed on Patrick, so Nancy bent over and gave him a kiss. Patrick went next, but he didn't have much luck because the bottle ended on boys twice in a row. When he finally spun the bottle on a girl, it was Holly, and he tried to give her a French kiss.

"No! No way!" shouted Holly, pushing back from his enthusiastic embrace. "I hardly even know you, and I'm certainly not going to kiss like that." Holly was evidently upset that Patrick would try something like that with her boyfriend, Tom, around.

"That's OK," replied an only slightly embarrassed Patrick. "Kissing like that is a good way to get better acquainted."

"Well then, try it on someone else!" Holly yelled, as Tom sat back, laughing.

And so, the game went on. Emboldened by Patrick, every time the boys spun the bottle on a girl, they tried to kiss her in the French style. Most times the chosen girl resisted but perhaps not with as much force as Holly had.

My first two times with the bottle, it landed on girls I either didn't know or didn't care about. On my third spin, however, the bottle landed on Susan. Following the others, I tried to give her a French kiss. And guess what? She kissed right back! I was elated! I was the first boy at the party to pull off a French kiss! I even beat out Craig, who just couldn't get the bottle to land on Nancy.

"Damn you, Sonny!" our leader shouted with a grin. "How can you have all the luck? You don't even like girls, but look at you now!"

I blushed, but couldn't think of a good reply. Susan also reddened, but had nothing to say.

My French kiss with Susan marked the highlight of the party for me. Ten minutes later, we heard the upstairs door open, and the twins' parents stuck their heads down in the basement.

"Hello? We're back!" called out the father, peering around to make sure that everything was in order. "Is everyone having a good time?'

"Oh, Daddy, I'm glad you're back," replied Nancy, thinking back to Grant's unwanted intrusion. "But why did you return early? I thought you'd promised not to come back until *after* the party?"

"Oh, my Lord! Did we promise that? I'm sorry; we must have forgotten." The father smiled, looking back to his wife for support.

"Oh yes!" The mom laughed. "We must not have been listening."

Either the parents were pulling a fast one here or maybe they *had* really forgotten what they'd promised. No one could figure out the true story. Given Grant's unwanted appearance, most of us were probably happy to see them return. But at least some of us boys were now having fun trying to kiss like the French. Unfortunately, we had to abandon these efforts once the parents returned.

I had a wonderful time at the party and really enjoyed my time with Susan. She was a great girl who seemed to put up with all my insecurities. But after the party ended and I was back home, I decided that I just wasn't ready to be part of a couple: girlfriends just took too much time and effort. You always had to be thinking of things to do with them. Every night you had to call them on the phone and be ready with some cute story. If you didn't have a tall tale to tell, then you had to invent something on the spot. You also had to plan to do things with them on the weekends, and then your buddies in the gang would tease you for leaving them behind. And what in the world would you do with your girlfriend at school when all her friends were around? How would you break in on the little girlie groups? Finally, if you ever started walking around the halls holding hands, all the kids would begin talking. That was the worst of the worst: to be the object of all that gossip.

Craig might be ready to deal with all the hassles of having and maintaining a girlfriend, but I certainly wasn't.

CHAPTER 16

It was now Easter, and people were saying that Todd was back in town. None of us had seen him, and I couldn't see any possible connection between the two events. Todd was the last person to celebrate Easter or any other kind of religious holiday. He was a bad boy and a heathen through and through. Craig and I were the only boys I knew who went to church, and it didn't seem to do us much good. Neither of us wanted to tell the truth about the awful things that we had done.

Rumor had it that Todd had returned home to see his mom and his buddy Grant. The "seeing Grant" part may have been true, because we began to hear stories about what the two boys were doing. Some said they were egging cars again. Others said that they had bought BB guns and were shooting out streetlights. The best story, however, came from Danny, who heard it from his older brother Alan.

"Did you hear the latest about Todd and Grant?" chuckled Danny one morning on our way to school.

"No," I replied, somewhat afraid to ask. "What have those two been up to?"

"They've been breaking into Chucky's and stealing beer and wine," Danny continued, smiling broadly. "You know Chucky's, that mom-and-pop store on the main drag in Preston."

"Oh, that's bullshit," said Craig, incredulously. "How could they do that without getting caught?"

"I don't know for sure," said Danny, "but I heard they found a key to the back door of the store, and they've been breaking in late at night."

"But how could they do that without the owners finding out?" I asked.

"My brother says that the owners have discovered that stuff is missing, but they're not sure who's doing it."

"So, what are they going to do about it?" sniffed Craig.

"Well, my brother says that the police are keeping a close eye on the store at night so they can see if they can catch anyone."

Sure enough, several days later we heard a story about Grant being caught by the police late at night with stolen beer in his possession. Grant was underage, so he was probably going to get charged with both possessing liquor as a minor and trafficking in stolen goods. But we didn't hear anything about Todd. Maybe he was just better at running away.

The story about Grant being in police custody got us all worried again. If the police pressed Grant, and Grant confessed to everything he'd done, then maybe he'd spill the beans on us. And then we'd be called up and interviewed by the police. They'd pull the truth out of us by one means or the other, and then pack us off to jail.

We sweated our situation for a couple of days, but Grant must have kept quiet. No one appeared at our door, and we had no unwelcome phone calls from the police.

The Saturday before Easter was a warm and beautiful day, the first real day of spring. Craig and I were playing catch in the park. Dressed in shorts and short-sleeves, we were tossing the ball back and forth, dreaming out loud about summer baseball. For once it seemed like we didn't have a care in the world.

Out of the corner of my eye I noticed a red Ford Mustang cruising slowly around the park. I didn't pay it much attention because I didn't know anyone who had a car and drove. But suddenly, without warning, an unwanted voice from within the Mustang called out to us: "Hey, guys! What have you been up to?" It was Todd.

"Hell," muttered Craig under his breath. "It's that damn troublemaker, Todd. Let's pretend like we don't hear him."

However, after all these months Todd was more than anxious to talk. When we ignored his first call, he simply stopped the car and hollered out again: "Guys, are you trying to ignore me? Now, that wouldn't be nice. Come on over here, and let's catch up."

We had little choice, so the two of us walked slowly over to his car. I could feel my palms beginning to sweat and my heart beating faster.

"Where've you been all this time?" Craig asked in a careful voice.

"Oh, I've been living with my dad. He lives in another state. But all the time I've been there I've been thinking about you guys. So how are you doing?"

"Oh, we're doing fine," replied Craig, quite warily.

"Grant tells me that you've been cool and haven't been talking to the cops," Todd said. "That's good—I'm proud of you."

"I guess we didn't have much choice," Craig observed.

"Hey, I'll tell you what," proposed Todd, clearly anxious to break through this frosty reception. "How about if you hop in and we take a drive around town? Then we can talk more freely."

I knew that the last thing either of us wanted to do was to get into a car with Todd. Both of us were genuinely afraid of this crazy boy who did all kinds of evil things. And I was thinking to myself, *Where in the world did this guy ever get a car? I bet he doesn't even have a driver's license!*

Craig must have been thinking similar thoughts when he replied, "I'm not sure if we want to drive around. And anyway," he added, "where did you get a car like this?"

"Oh, don't worry about that," Todd replied in a cool and even voice. "It's my dad's car, and he lets me drive it around. Come on—hop in."

"Oh, I'm not sure if we want to," said Craig, speaking for both of us.

"I *said*, hop in," growled our tormentor, this time in a far more direct tone. "Now."

When Todd talked like this, we had little choice. He was twice as big as us and probably three times as strong. So, quite unwillingly, the two of us climbed into his car, Craig sitting in the front and me in the back.

We circled the park and then took a left onto the main road toward Preston. Todd stepped on the gas and quickly got the car moving above the speed limit. Then he turned and grinned his crooked smile at Craig. "Now, isn't this more comfortable?" Craig stayed silent, so our erstwhile friend rambled on, "How about if we head for the cliffs outside of town?"

There were two sets of impressive, but isolated, cliffs on the other side of town that looked out over the surrounding countryside. All the high school kids with cars would head out there on Friday night with their dates. I'd never been out there myself, but I didn't know about Craig.

"How about if we just cruise around Preston?" our leader countered, obviously anxious to avoid being caught in any lonely spot with this guy.

"But then we can't drink any of the liquor that I have stashed out by the cliffs," responded Todd. "Don't you want to drink some while we talk?"

"Nah, that's OK. We're cool right now."

But Todd had the wheel and was in charge, so he could easily ignore our wishes. He stepped on the gas again and sped on out to the cliffs to check on his stash. And to talk.

For all his bluster, when we arrived at the cliffs, we discovered that Todd really didn't have much alcohol stored away: only a six-pack of luke-warm beer and half a bottle of cheap red wine. Apparently unwilling to part with the wine, he handed each of us a beer. "Cheer up, guys," he urged, flashing a weird kind of half-smile. "It's the start of Easter vacation. Relax, and kick back a little."

"Thanks," we said in unison, accepting the beer gratefully.

Now I must admit that I didn't like being with Todd, but I did very much enjoy the beer. At this point in my life, alcohol of any kind was a real treat. My parents were teetotalers, so they kept no alcohol at home and were always trying to drum into my head the evils of drink. However, I was sure that a beer or two would never hurt—especially on occasions like this.

"Yep, you know I don't have much to do at my dad's," Todd added as soon as we started drinking. "I don't know anyone out there and so I've been doing a lot of thinking."

"About what?"

"I've been thinking about you guys and the accident," he said. "And you know where I think we went wrong?"

"No," said Craig, looking up puzzled.

"Well, we put the manhole cover down on the railroad track all wrong. We should've made sure the cover was sitting flat on the track, rather than on an angle."

"Well, hell!" yelled Craig, suddenly exploding in anger. "You were the one who told us what to do! Why didn't you put the cover down like that? You told us you'd done it a bunch of times before with Grant. And that nothing had ever gone wrong!"

"But Grant and me always put the cover down flat on the rail. With you guys I thought that it would be neat to experiment a little."

"Oh great," responded Craig, still mad with the sarcasm dripping in his voice. "You decided to experiment, and it ended up killing one person and seriously hurting five others. That's just great."

"But hey, man, I didn't mean to kill that guy. It was all just an experiment," he repeated with emphasis. "If you don't try new things, then you'll never learn."

"But trying new things in a dangerous situation like that is just plain stupid," I ventured. The words tumbled out of my mouth a bit more critical than I had intended. But I wasn't all that concerned. I knew that neither of these two alpha males would pay me any heed.

"No, it's not at all stupid," Todd retorted, with much conviction. "Stupid's when you hurt yourself or your friends. Stupid is not when you hurt people you don't even know. Or care about."

Neither Craig nor I could think of a response to this. Todd obviously had a very different way of looking at the world. In his world, everything was all black and white, with no grays. People were either his friends and with him, or his enemies and against him. He deemed all the people he didn't know to be against him. Maybe with his great physical strength Todd could enforce a world like that, but I knew that I couldn't. And I suspected that Craig couldn't, either. I think that both of us considered people we didn't know to be possible friends.

After a minute of uncomfortable silence, Craig tried a new track with Todd. "Look, lots of people think that what we did out there on the railroad track was wrong, dead wrong. Look at all the cops and school administrators who keep questioning us, trying to find out what happened."

"Oh hell, you can't worry about those rule followers and do-gooders," retorted Todd without batting an eye. "Those kinds of people are always looking around to do good. If you do anything wrong in this world, you just have to forget it and move on. As long as you and your friends are OK, then everything's fine."

"But don't you ever worry about the bad things you do to other people?" I asked very quietly.

"No, not at all."

With that the three of us fell silent again. I felt disappointed but not surprised by the direction our conversation had taken. Todd clearly moved and acted on different principles than we did, and that was no surprise.

In the silence that ensued I began worrying about a whole bunch of unconnected things. I started worrying about Todd's messed-up view of the world, and where that would lead us. *But hell,* I thought in my head, *what can I really do about Todd's perverted world view? I'm not his mother. Or his father.* That led me to a much more immediate concern: How were we going to get home? *Drinking beer out here is all well and fine, but how are we ever going to get this no-good hoodlum to drive us back home? He might just leave us out here forever.* And that led me back to my greatest fear in life: getting beat up. *What if Todd decides to beat us up and leave us out here in the middle of nowhere? What will we do then?*

Craig must have been mulling over similar things, because right after finishing his beer he asked quite pointedly, "Todd, do you think you can drive us back to the park? I've really got to be home by five."

"Why do you need to be back so early?" shot back our nemesis.

"I need to get back for dinner."

"OK," replied Todd, in a grudging, but not totally unfriendly, manner. "I'll drive you back. It's fun hanging out with you guys, but I need to get back, too."

But Todd must have sensed that he had an advantage here, because he quickly added, almost like a planned afterthought: "But before we go, I need to ask you something."

"What's that?" Craig asked in a very guarded tone.

"Would you guys like to join me in a little adventure Monday night? I've got some money to pick up, and Grant's too busy to come. How about if you guys join me for a little support?"

CHAPTER 17

I'll never be able to explain why Craig agreed to meet Todd that Monday night. I was sure that Craig feared—and maybe even hated—Todd. I was certainly frightened by the guy and didn't want to spend a single extra moment around him. The only explanation that I can think of is that somehow our leader was mesmerized by Todd and wanted to figure out what made him tick. Craig was like that; he was always pathologically interested in the bad boys and finding out what made them do such crazy things. And Todd certainly did insane stuff, way beyond what Craig ever dreamed up.

And me? Why the hell did I go? Well, it was a dumb decision, but I just decided to tag along with Craig. I had nothing else to do that night, and Craig asked me several times to come along. I was always a good follower. While I was certainly scared of Todd, I figured that as long as Craig was around, everything would be OK. If things got too dicey, I could always run on home.

Right at seven, Todd pulled up in his bright red Ford Mustang. I was still wondering how he could have a flashy car like this. As far as I knew, Todd had never worked a day in his life. And I really doubted if his dad ever would have trusted him with an expensive car like this. *Dads just didn't do that*, I said to myself. *He must have stolen the car. That's how he gets everything else. He never could've gotten a Mustang on his own.*

"Hey, guys, thanks for coming," Todd said as we jumped in.

Heck, something must be up, I thought as we arranged ourselves like before: Craig in the front and me in the back. *Todd never thanks anyone for anything. He must want us to do something really bad.*

"Where are we going?" asked Craig, anxious at the start to clarify things.

"Well, here's the deal," Todd explained. "I have to go to a house in Preston to pick up fifty bucks that some guys owe me. I brought them some liquor from the store, and they still haven't paid up."

"What store?" Craig asked, undoubtedly thinking back to the story we'd heard about Todd and Grant stealing from Chucky's.

"Oh hell. You guys don't need to know that," Todd replied, smiling tightly. "I just got the liquor—that's all you need to know."

"Well, how about these guys you're visiting," Craig pressed. "Do you know them?"

"No, not really. That's why I brought this along, just in case," said Todd, yanking up his shirt to reveal a small pistol tucked in his pants.

"Holy hell!" yelled Craig, recoiling back immediately. "Don't tell me you have a gun!" This was the first time that either of us had seen someone with a gun. We'd seen people carrying guns all the time on TV, but this was real life—not some fake police show.

"Yeah, and what's wrong with that? Actually, it's not mine."

"Whose is it, then?"

"It belongs to Grant," Todd replied.

Todd just can't tell the truth, I said quietly to myself. *Here he is playing the classic game of blaming his best friend for his own stupidity and bad judgment. I bet he's either borrowed or stolen the pistol from another one of his hooligan friends.*

"But why do you need a gun?" I piped up, trying to insert myself into the conversation. "Are these guys really that bad?"

"I don't know—maybe. Grant knows them better than me, and he said that they might be trouble."

"What kind of trouble?" I asked nervously.

"Well, let's just say that they're always dealing in goods. And sometimes they don't pay up like they should."

"Dealing in goods? And not paying? What does that even mean?" shouted a by now very agitated Craig. "Do you mean that they steal stuff?"

But Todd went silent. With no reply coming, our leader began muttering under his breath, "Hell, this looks like a goddamn mess."

Craig was obviously having second thoughts about this whole adventure. And so was I. I was hoping that our leader would take charge and do something. Fast. Like flinging open the car door so that both of us could bolt away. But when I tried to catch Craig's eye, to see if he wanted to run, he looked away. Like he was still deciding what in the world to do.

"Aw, relax," said Todd, doing his best to calm us down. "Don't worry. I'll do all the work. All you guys need to do is sit tight in the car and wait for me. And keep an eye on things. It will all be easy."

"But what happens if something goes wrong?"

"Nothing will go wrong," Todd said with a growl. "You guys just stay cool and leave all the thinking to me."

But the last time we did that, I muttered to myself, *one person got killed and five people were seriously hurt. Why are we supposed to trust you again?*

The house was a dilapidated two-story wooden structure with a porch in a sketchy part of Preston. True to his word, Todd left us in the car. He went up and banged on the door. When no one appeared, he tried peering in one of the side windows. After about five minutes of off-and-on rapping on the window and door, a single light came on inside. A scruffy-looking character appeared at the door, cracking it open a bit to listen to what Todd had to say. The two obviously didn't know or trust each other. The guy finally nodded his head slightly and let Todd slip inside.

During his absence Craig and I nervously fidgeted around in the car, wondering what in the hell to do. Neither of us wanted to serve as lookouts for some madman armed with a gun. But neither of us had a good alternative plan.

"Hell, this is really scary," I moaned. "Do you think we ought to run?"

"I don't know," Craig replied, sounding very uneasy. "I really don't know where we are. Where could we run to?"

"I have no idea."

"Which way is the main drag?" Craig asked.

"I don't know."

"Then maybe we should just sit and wait. What else can we do?"

So, the two of us remained sitting in the car in a rundown part of Preston, fearfully watching the house as it grew dark. Running away in this area of town at dusk seemed like a bad idea—even for two teenagers who were anxious to flee anywhere.

Ten or fifteen minutes passed before Todd reappeared on the porch by himself. He walked briskly back to the car, looking mighty pleased with himself.

"Wow, after a shaky start, that turned out OK. At first, they tried to play dumb and claimed that they didn't know anything about the booze. But after I showed them the gun, they suddenly remembered everything real fast." He smiled as he recounted his bravado inside the house. "*And I got the money. But let's get out of here before they have any second thoughts. They weren't at all happy when I left.*"

Holy hell! I thought to myself. *What have we gotten ourselves into? Todd sticks up people in a house and then leaves before they can find their own guns. What's going to happen next!*

Todd started the car and pulled away from the curb with a squeal. At the first intersection we stopped for the light to change. There was almost no traffic on the street, and Todd seemed ecstatic that we were making such a quick escape. "Damn, that wasn't too hard," he said, smiling broadly and banging his fist on the steering wheel for emphasis. "Maybe I should do that more often."

Just as soon as Todd finished congratulating himself, a police cruiser with flashing red lights pulled up right behind us. Maybe the cruiser had been sitting there waiting for us the whole time. Or maybe it was just watching the neighborhood. It was impossible to tell. In any event, the cruiser was on us with absolutely no warning.

"Oh shit!" yelled Todd, hitting the steering wheel again, this time in total anger. "What the hell is this?"

Before he could answer his own question, Todd revved the engine and shot through the red light. The cruiser turned on its siren and gave chase. Todd turned left down one side street and right down the next. The cruiser, with siren blaring, followed right behind. Half a mile down the second street, Todd suddenly veered over to the side of the road. Killing the engine, he leaped out of the vehicle and began running for his life towards the woods. With his long legs he had a good fifty-yard head start before one of the two policemen jumped out of the cruiser and started giving chase. Todd was obviously well practiced at the art of running from the law.

While this unfolded, Craig and I sat motionless in the car. We were rooted by fear. Never before had either of us been stopped by a police cruiser or anything else connected with the law.

The second policeman got out of his car. Approaching us carefully from behind, he yelled, "Get out of the car slowly with your hands up!"

We did as he commanded. We were terrified.

"Now spread your legs and bend over, touching the car. Keep your hands up and out of your pockets."

The cop patted us down. Craig first and then me. He emptied our pockets, taking a small penknife from Craig and two sticks of gum from me. Neither of us was carrying wallets.

After placing the contents of our pockets on the hood of the car, the cop shined a bright flashlight into our eyes. Seeing that we weren't hardened criminals, but rather two very frightened teenagers, he relaxed a bit before asking, "What are you boys doing riding around in a stolen car?"

"Officer," replied Craig in a trembling voice, "we just got into the car. We had no idea that it was stolen."

"Do you have any identification?"

"No, we don't," Craig said, speaking in a quivering voice for both of us.

"Well, do you know who the driver of the car was?"

"Yes, it was Todd Banks," I answered, speaking up for the first time.

"Is this Mr. Banks a friend of yours?"

"Oh no, officer. We barely know him," I said.

"If you barely know him, why did you get into the car with him?"

"He was just giving us a ride into Preston," replied Craig.

"Don't you have any other way of getting around?"

"No, sir."

And so, the questioning went on, without yielding much more additional information. We knew nothing about the car or where it had come from. We also knew nothing about why we had come to this particular house in Preston or who lived there. We didn't even know where Todd was staying in town, other than with his mom. But the policeman probably knew all this already: he didn't write down any of our responses, and he didn't call anything in to headquarters.

It was definitely dark when the other cop returned about fifteen minutes later. He was breathing heavily and his face was beet-red. But he returned empty-handed: no Todd. Our bad-boy friend must have escaped into the woods.

The two policemen put us in the back of their cruiser and took us down to the station. They made us sit in a holding cell before recording our names, addresses, and phone numbers in a thick black ledger.

I was scared to death that the police would put us in a cell overnight. Or call our parents and have them come bail us out. Either way, I'd be in a whole new heap of trouble. My friends would start calling me "juvenile delinquent," and my dad would beat the holy hell out of me. I would get grounded for a year of weekends.

But after a huddled conference in the back of the station, the sergeant in charge stepped forward to address us: "Do you boys know that this Todd Banks is a wanted juvenile?"

"No, sir," gulped Craig.

"He's wanted on charges of breaking and entering, theft, and possession of stolen goods. And he's also wanted on charges of carrying a concealed weapon."

"We didn't know any of that, officer," added Craig.

"Well, now you do," continued the sergeant. "If you ever see this Todd Banks again, you have to report that contact to us as soon as possible. Is that understood?"

"Yes, officer."

"You can go now. But I warn you in no uncertain terms: stay away from Todd Banks. He is nothing but trouble."

We never did see Todd again on that Easter break. It was like he'd vanished into thin air. Some people said he'd gone to Canada, while others said he'd moved to California; a few even claimed that he'd escaped to Alaska. But all these stories seemed absurd to me. More than likely, I figured, he just went back to living with his dad. But if he did that, *then why didn't the police in that state—wherever that was—go pick him up?* I could never understand that. Maybe the police didn't share information on wanted juveniles across state lines. Or maybe they just figured that they could catch him whenever and wherever they wanted. Todd had a "Wanted" sign on his forehead, and soon enough they'd catch him somewhere.

Todd's friend Grant got sent back to reform school. Or at least that's what we heard from Danny's brother. Reform school, and all the bad things that happened there, were something we never discussed. The reform school was located in another part of the state, so even Craig didn't know anyone there. And we knew even less about what bad boys like Grant had to do in reform school. Danny's brother claimed that the authorities made them smash up boulders into smaller rocks to help build roads, but that sounded like another made-up story to me. Everyone knew that only the worst convicts at San Quentin had to do that.

CHAPTER 18

Our town had two sets of cliffs. The larger and more impressive set was on the other side of Preston, and way too far to walk to; these were the cliffs that Todd had driven us to. The smaller set was located much closer to town, about an hour's walk north along the railroad line. Part of this second set of cliffs overlooked a wide and fast-flowing stream.

One Saturday in late spring, Craig decided that we just had to hike over and see if it was time to go diving from the smaller cliffs. This was always a rather tricky proposition. It had to be late enough in spring so that the water in the stream wasn't ice cold, but it also had to be before summer began, because then there usually wasn't enough water for diving. Rumor had it that a boy had been seriously injured a couple of years ago when he dived from the cliffs and the water was too shallow. He'd broken his neck when he hit the rocks on the bottom of the stream.

The four of us started out for the cliffs one warm May afternoon. Mike was with us this time, and we were all looking forward to a fun day of jumping into the water. We wore shorts and old tennis shoes. The shoes were important, because the stream bed was sharp and it was easy to cut your feet on the bottom.

"Hey, guys!" shouted Craig, barely able to contain his enthusiasm. "This year I'm going to dive from the very top of the cliffs. I bet that none of you will try that."

"My ass," replied Danny. "No one's ever done that. I bet you'll chicken out by the time we get there."

"Wanna bet on it?" yelled Craig, always ready to wager money on his crazy dares.

"No, this time I'll just watch you chicken out," said Danny, who was probably low on funds.

Although this was my first trip to the cliffs in warm weather, I had seen the diving area in the fall. In my mind, diving from halfway up the cliffs was frightening enough, but diving from the top seemed downright suicidal. From halfway up it was maybe a twenty-five-foot plunge into the water, but from the top it was more than forty feet.

When we reached the cliffs, we were surprised to find two other boys already there. These boys, bigger and older, seemed to be having a wonderful time: whooping and hollering and carrying on as they dove into the water from about halfway up the cliff.

When one of these boys bobbed up from a dive, Danny shouted, "Grant! Is that you?"

"Yeah, it's me," answered Grant as he slowly pulled himself from the water. "Who did you think it was, Santa Claus? Hey, guys," he continued, smiling slowly as it dawned on him who we were. "Long time no see. How are you doing?"

"We're fine," stumbled Danny. "But we heard that you were back in reform school."

"Well, they did send me to reform school for a while. But they just couldn't keep me there long," he chuckled. "And so now I'm back."

"But how'd you get out so fast?" Craig asked.

"Oh well, let's just say that my dad helped me out. But let's not talk about that."

Grant's father was a local lawyer and a fixture in the community. Some people claimed that he was an alcoholic and a ne'er-do-well, just like his son, but he'd seemed like an ordinary guy to me the couple of times I'd run into him in the streets. He was always smartly dressed, and I never noticed him hanging around the only tavern in town.

Grant added, "What are you guys doing here? Did you come to dive?"

"I don't know," answered Danny, trying to cover for us all. "We wanted to check out the cliffs, but we might not stay."

"Well, I really think you should stay," Grant urged. "You guys have done a good job keeping quiet about everything. And now you can have some fun."

Now, the last thing I wanted to do was to stay and "have fun" with Grant and his friend. And my three buddies must have felt pretty much the same way, because I heard Craig whisper quietly, "Shit, this looks like trouble. We need to get out of here."

But Grant pressed us to stay. When his initial pleas didn't have much effect, he began taunting us: "What are you guys afraid of?" and "Only girlie-girls are scared of diving here; even my little sister dives from these cliffs." And finally, "I could dive from here blindfolded."

At first, the four of us stayed quiet, refusing to take the bait. We all knew that Grant was just trying to get under our skin and make us stay. But Craig could never stay quiet when someone else was putting him down. He always wanted to be top-dog, not someone's step-dog. So, after a couple of minutes of Grant's challenges and reproaches, he caved in.

"OK, we'll stay for a couple of minutes. But we won't do anything crazy."

Our leader probably gave in because diving into the cold water looked so inviting on this beautiful spring day. We had already walked all this way to go diving. And out here in the woods, it didn't seem like the bad boy Grant could make us do anything really stupid or dangerous. We could always run away if things got too dicey.

"Come on, guys!" shouted Grant, pleased that he'd gotten his way. "I'll show you how it's done."

So, the four of us followed him to a ledge about halfway up the cliffs.

"The trick," Grant rattled on, "is to land in the deep pool of water that's about fifteen feet from shore. It's too shallow closer to shore, and landing any further out is dangerous because of all the rocks. Watch me! I'll show you the perfect dive."

Now the last thing that any of us wanted to hear was Grant's self-serving explanations.

Craig and Danny already knew how to dive from these cliffs. And Mike and I didn't want to hear any of this boasting, either, because neither of us believed anything Grant had to say. We all knew Grant was just a total show-off.

Grant and his friend strutted over to the edge. Grant dove first; he went in headfirst and landed perfectly. His friend followed and did the same. Then Craig and Danny jumped; both of them chose the safer feet-first method of entry. I followed their lead and was very happy to land right in the middle of the deep pool. Mike jumped last, and he also went in feet first. Compared to Grant and his friend, the four of us seemed like total wussies.

"OK, guys," urged Grant, smiling his lopsided grin. "Since you're here, let's try something more challenging. Let's try jumping from the top of the cliff!"

"Have you ever done that before?" asked Craig, clearly skeptical. Now that he was at the cliffs and jumping, our leader didn't seem to be nearly as confident as before. In fact, he now seemed more than a little scared. Maybe Grant's presence had sucked away all of his braggadocio. Grant could certainly do that to you: he was always so big and loud and damn right sure of himself.

"Of course. Sam and I have done it a bunch of times."

"Yeah, it's a blast," chimed in Sam, a boy I'd never met before. He had curly blond hair and was a lot thinner than Grant. He lacked his buddy's height and powerful build. Sam also seemed quieter and willing to follow Grant to the ends of the earth. Just like we followed Craig around.

Grant and Sam scampered up to the top of the cliff. Craig and Danny followed. But Mike and I remained where we were by the stream: the two of us wanted no part of this insanity.

Grant dove first from the top of the forty-foot ledge. With his thick and muscular torso, he looked like an out-of-place wrestler decked out in a skimpy bathing suit. On his Olympic-like dive he stretched out his arms in midflight and landed headfirst right in the middle of the deep pool.

"Wow, that was awesome," he shouted just as soon as he surfaced. Grant was always his best cheerleader.

Sam went next. He jumped feet first and held his arms tightly at his side. He just didn't have the same presence or pizazz as his buddy. I began to wonder if he'd ever done this dive before.

Craig followed and dove into the water the same way Sam had. It was obvious that this was Craig's first time diving from the top. His face was white and tense, and he held his arms clasped rigidly to his side the whole way down. He didn't look like he was having fun.

Danny was the last of the four to go. He stood up there an awfully long time, staring down into the water like he was searching for the courage to jump. Finally, he leaped feet first. I said a silent prayer for him the whole way down. From the look on his face, he was terrified.

"OK, Sonny and Mike!" hollered Grant. "Now it's your turn to dive. You can either dive headfirst like me, or feet first like these pansies." Grant had no fear and seemed to delight in needling people who had a greater respect for death.

"There's no way I'm going to dive," I stammered. "I really don't want to die just yet."

"Me, either," chimed in Mike, the youngest one there.

"Ah, you two are just weenies. You ought to be shot," Grant yelled.

"My little sister has more guts than you," Sam added. "And she's only 10 years old."

Grant and Sam jumped from the top again, and then they began to ramp up the pressure on Mike and me. Grant was a master at this; he'd probably learned the skill from Todd. Both of them were huge physical specimens who excelled at tormenting smaller boys.

"You two are a bunch of pussies," yelled Grant, for probably the third time. "Why won't you jump? What are you afraid of?"

"It's just…it's just too high," Mike stuttered.

"Look here!" shouted Grant. "If you two don't get moving to the top right now, I'm going to carry you up there myself."

Grant was certainly large and strong enough to carry out his threat. He could easily carry one or both of us on his hip up to the top. And being the unpredictable sort, there was no telling what he might do to us up there. For kicks, he just might decide to pants us and then toss us naked and butt-first into the water. Who knew how or where we would land then?

"OK, OK," I replied miserably, as Grant moved in, glaring. "I'll jump if Mike comes, too."

"What choice do I have?" Mike grumbled glumly. There was no place for him—or any of us—to run.

With Grant at our heels, Mike and I trudged up slowly to the top of the cliff. Craig and Danny stood at the bottom quietly watching. They seemed to enjoy seeing us get pushed around by this giant.

At the top I crossed myself, closed my eyes, and said a quick prayer. And then I jumped. It seemed like an eternity before I hit the cold, moving water. But at least I was alive when I surfaced, and there was no blood and nothing felt broken.

It took Mike a much longer time to leap. He kept staring down at the water and muttering to himself. For a time, I thought that Grant was going to push him; Mike seemed that terrified and rooted to the spot. But at last he jumped. Since he was so tense, however, Mike misjudged his landing. He jumped just a little too far out into the stream.

"Aw shit!" he cried just as soon as he surfaced. "I hit my leg on the bottom, and now it really hurts!"

Craig and Danny, watching from the shore at the bottom, quickly swam out and pulled him to the shore. Mike couldn't stand, and his left leg was straight and limp. His ankle was black and blue and all twisted up, and he was screaming at the top of his lungs: "Shit! Help! It hurts! It *really* hurts!"

Craig and Danny bent down and examined the ankle. "Yeah, it looks pretty bad. It looks like it's broken," yelled Craig, who had some experience with broken bones.

"Of course, it's broken!" screamed our friend. "It hurts like hell!"

"Ah it doesn't look that bad to me," countered Grant, just as soon as he was able to get a good look at the ankle. "I don't see any bone poking through. Can you walk?"

"Of course I can't walk! It hurts like hell!" screamed Mike. "Help!"

Mike couldn't stand, so he continued to lie down on the rocky shore. He kept yelling and screaming like there was no tomorrow. There was no calming him down; this time even Craig couldn't hush him up.

After about ten minutes, Grant must have gotten tired of all the commotion. So, he barked out to his friend, "Sam, get over here! This guy just won't stop yelling. We're going to have to carry him out of here to get help."

"How are we going to do that?" replied the until now perfectly silent Sam.

"You grab his arms, and I'll grab his legs. We'll carry him out to the road piggyback style."

And so, Grant and Sam somehow carted the screaming Mike out of the woods. They piggybacked him about a half mile over the railroad tracks to the nearest road. There Danny and Craig flagged down a car and took him to the hospital. It turned out that he'd broken both his ankle and his shinbone on the rocks: he would have to spend two whole nights in the hospital.

So, Mike was the second member of our band to get a cast.

"Ah, what the hell," observed Craig on our next walk to school. "Broken bones seem to be a badge of honor around here. Those who try the hardest always seem to break something."

Fortunately, Mike wasn't with us that day on our walk to school, or he might have gotten really mad and hit Craig. While he was definitely a momma's boy and usually didn't have much spunk, when cornered in a tight place Mike could show a temper. Now that he'd been bitten by a dog

<u>and</u> broken his ankle jumping off a cliff—both at the urging of others—Mike seemed like he might be ready to explode at Craig. He might even have broken our leader's jaw.

CHAPTER 19

After our disastrous experience at homecoming, I decided that I was totally through with dances: parties like those at the twins' house were fine, but dances were simply too much trouble. When they were held at school, you had to wrack your brains about who to invite, plot out how to ask the girl, and then invent things to talk about. It was much too embarrassing. And then there was always the possibility that Craig might decide to do something crazy, and then you'd have to face Mr. Fagan all over again.

Now, Craig and I were sometime attenders of our local church. We usually went whenever our mothers got together and decided that we needed to go. Those Sundays usually coincided with times of the year when we were grounded or otherwise in trouble. I guess that our moms thought that a little church would help us see the error of our ways.

Craig and I also occasionally went to our church's youth group. We rarely attended the group's religious meetings, but we did show up periodically for their social activities. These activities were usually organized by two ninth-grade girls who had a good sense of what appealed to kids our age. So rather than putting on hayrides at Halloween or canoe trips in the spring, they favored things like limbo-stick parties in the fall and spring dances at the end of school.

In late May, Craig and I heard that the church group was planning its usual spring dance at the beginning of June. I had absolutely no desire to go, but Craig began his usual lobbying.

"We haven't been to a dance since homecoming," he reminded me, three or four times. "And so, we really have to go to this one."

"But hell," I objected. "I hate dances. And I really and truly don't want to go to any more of them."

"Oh, Sonny, lighten up," Craig urged, on our walk home from school one day. "Dances are a lot of fun. I'll help you out. If you don't want to ask Susan, then I'll find another date for you."

Craig must have sensed that Susan was a sensitive topic for me. While I had really enjoyed my time with her at the party, I hadn't said a word to her since then. Whenever I passed her in the halls, she always flashed me that "I'm hurt" look that I just didn't know how to deal with. I was too shy to march up and engage in any simple chit-chat. What would we have ever said? And I surely didn't want to apologize. As far as I could figure, I hadn't done anything wrong. At base, I guess that I was just clueless around girls. No wonder I had so many problems dealing with them.

"But it all sounds so difficult," I replied to Craig, carefully trying to hide my innermost feelings. "I certainly don't want to go with Susan, and I *really* don't want to go with anyone else. And anyway," I added with a half-smile, "how can you ask someone else for me? That's just way *too* weird!"

"Oh hell, don't worry about that," he reassured me. "I'm sure I can arrange something."

Our leader was nothing if not self-assured around girls.

Four or five days later on our way to school, Craig announced: "Sonny, it's all arranged. You're going to go to the church dance with Eve, and I'm going with Dana. It should be great fun!"

"Who the hell is Eve?" I responded, totally befuddled. "Do I even know her?"

"Oh, sure you do. She's the short, brown-haired girl with glasses who's always hanging around Dana."

Now Dana I knew: she was slim and tall and one of the most outgoing girls in our class. But Eve? I really couldn't recall any brown-haired girl with glasses hanging around Dana. Was I missing something?

"Do you want me to introduce you?" Craig added. "That might be good, because she's kind of quiet."

Sure enough, at lunch that day Craig hauled me over to a tableful of giggling girls and introduced me to my future date. Craig was in his element here, easily parrying back and forth with all the girls around the table. But for me it was a very awkward and unsettling experience. I had nothing to say to any of the laughing girls, and when I was introduced to Eve, I realized that, yes, she did exist. However, she was one of the most painfully shy girls in the whole eighth grade. She had beautiful brown curly hair, but when I stuck my hand out to greet her, all I got in return (with no handshake) was, "Hi. You must be Sonny."

Tongue-tied teenager that I was, I couldn't think of any witty reply except, "Yes, I am."

Eve had nothing else to add, so our introduction ended right then and there. No smile, no handshake, and certainly no small talk.

On this basis, the two of us hooked up as dates to the dance.

Craig decided that we should double date and that his mom would drive us to the church. Happily, the dance was an informal affair, so we didn't need to dress up. I guess that Eve found out all the details from Dana, who knew the organizers of the event, because I sure didn't call her with any information. I didn't even know her number.

The dance was held in our church's huge basement, which was large enough to accommodate two basketball courts end to end. The basement was a cavernous affair, with concrete columns in the middle and at the ends and a ceiling that stretched up several floors. On the second floor there were paneled rooms with glass windows that looked out onto the whole open area.

Only the front part of the basement was being used for the dance; large, wooden partitions separated the dance floor from the "no go" other parts of the basement. No band was on hand, but the organizers had installed a record player in one corner and several speakers next to the columns around the basement. They had also strategically placed candles in glasses on small tables along the sides of the room.

When we arrived, four adult chaperones were standing awkwardly along the sidelines. Four or five couples were milling around the dance floor, but no one was out dancing. There was really no place for anyone to sit down.

Craig didn't like this arrangement, so he promptly marched off into the closed-off part of the basement to get four chairs. He smiled. "There, isn't that more comfortable?" as we settled into our seats, while everyone else remained standing.

"Oh, you're so resourceful!" beamed Dana, who was clearly impressed with her date. "You always take charge."

"I guess that's what I do. Someone has to."

Dana reached out and squeezed Craig's hand. From the glow on her face, she seemed to have a major crush on our leader. Until now, Craig had always been going out with Nancy, the twin, so I had no idea what was up. Maybe he and Nancy had had a fight, or maybe Craig just wanted to sample the field. You couldn't ever really tell with Craig. He was always moving here and there, and the girls always seemed to be lined up to go out with him. So maybe Dana was just the next, lucky one.

With Dana's encouragement, Craig set out to change other features of the dance. "Don't you think it's too bright in here?" he asked no one in particular. "How about if we turn off some of these lights and instead use more candles?"

"Sure, that's a great idea!" cooed Dana.

With some pleading, Craig convinced the chaperones to dim the lights and add more candles around the sides of the room. The dance floor suddenly became a lot darker and more inviting.

And then Craig started in on the music. When we entered, the record player was playing slow, mournful tunes like "Blue Velvet." Craig decided that we needed to liven things up by switching to a more modern rock and roll format. Right now, the Beatles were all the rage, and Craig announced that we just *had* to hear their latest songs. The people in charge kindly obliged by putting on Beatles tunes like "I Want to Hold Your Hand" and "She Loves You." For good measure, they also added in a few Herman's Hermits hits like "I'm into Something Good."

Craig and Dana took to the dance floor. Dana was all giggly, and on the faster songs she really let Craig swing her around. No one else was dancing, so they had the run of the floor. They were clearly having a terrific time swinging and dancing and laughing.

"Hey, Sonny!" cried Craig after the second song had ended. "Why don't you and Eve join us out here?"

Following Craig's urging, the two of us took to the floor. Eve danced in a manner quite unlike her vivacious friend; while Dana glided back and forth across the floor, Eve remained formal and stiff. She didn't even let me put my hand on her back. I was beginning to think that this might be a long night.

After two or three more records, several of the other couples standing on the sidelines joined us out on the floor. They seemed to like dancing to the sounds of the latest British rock stars. They danced in a comfortable middle-of-the-road style, somewhere between the giddy, carefree form of Craig and Dana and the more constrained style of Eve and me.

After one of the livelier songs, I heard Craig whisper to his date, "Do you want to go upstairs and make out?"

"OK," replied Dana, squeezing his hand again. For such a talkative and opinionated girl at school, Dana was really following all of Craig's leads tonight.

Craig's advance on Dana really caught me by surprise. Never before had I heard one of my friends ask a girl something like this. Craig was obviously trying to take advantage of Dana's crush on him. I began to wonder about where all this might end, especially in a church with so many chaperones around.

Craig and Dana disappeared from the basement for ten or fifteen minutes. In the meantime, Eve and I continued to dance. The organizers had run out of rock and roll records, and so they had gone back to some of the slower, more dated tunes. This made dancing with Eve even more awkward. But neither of us said anything as we moved about the floor, and we made no reference to our friends' departure.

Suddenly, at the end of one of the songs, all the lights in the basement flashed back on. One of the chaperones shouted out, "Fire! Fire! There's a fire upstairs!"

Sure enough, when we looked up, we could see flames through the windows of one of the paneled rooms on the second floor. At this point the fire appeared small and maybe containable. But it was definitely worrisome: everything in the rickety old church was made of wood. And the building hardly seemed prepared for any kind of an emergency. There were a couple of red fire extinguishers set along the walls, but they all looked ancient and never-used.

"Quick—everyone leave the basement *now!*" yelled another chaperone.

"I'll call the fire department!" someone else cried out.

Without delay, we grabbed our things and ran up and out of the basement. Only twenty or so of us were at the dance, so we all made it out without any problem. Two of the male chaperones stayed behind, trying to fight the fire with the decades-old extinguishers. But pretty soon they gave up and rushed to join us outside.

On the street I began looking around for Craig and Dana, but I couldn't spot them anywhere. Since I knew they'd been headed for the second floor, I got the sinking feeling that they might somehow be connected with the fire. I wasn't at all worried about their safety; I knew that Craig's quick wits would get him out of any jam. But I did worry that somehow his desire to push the limits had gotten him into trouble once again.

Within minutes we heard the sirens of the fire trucks. Two fire engines pulled up to us on the curb. And then there was more shouting, "Clear the way! Everyone, move across the street, away from the building!"

We crossed the street and watched the firemen go about their business. They hauled two large hoses up to the church and smashed several stained-glass windows to get better access to the fire. Then they began hosing down the growing flames. Thick plumes of smoke began to pour out of the windows of the old wooden church. It was impossible to see anything for many minutes.

But still no sign of our friends. It wasn't until the fire was out and the smoke had almost completely died away that Craig and Dana finally appeared. They were holding hands and looking very subdued. They were also covered from head to foot with dark, black soot.

"Where have you been?" I cried, running over to them. "We've been looking all over for you!"

"Let's say," stammered an ashen and very shaken Craig, "that we were on the second floor having some fun when all of a sudden this fire broke out. And then we had to run."

"But did you see how the fire started?"

"No, not at all. At first it was very dark. And then…*whoosh*…this fire started up. We have no idea how it began."

"But how come you're all covered with soot?"

"Let's just say," replied our leader, still all white and tensed up, "that we had trouble finding our way out. It was awfully dark in there."

"Yes, it was awfully dark and frightening in there," echoed the until-now silent Dana. She looked completely devastated.

Craig was not being truthful that night; in fact, he was being downright devious. But the truth always has a way of emerging. It wasn't until three or four days later that Craig finally fessed up.

It seems that on their way upstairs, Craig had decided that it would be "romantic" to take one of the candles with them "to light the way." When the two of them were making out, one of them—Craig was never clear on exactly who—knocked over the candle. The candle hit the ground and immediately lit up the carpet. Although they tried to stomp out the flame, the threadbare carpet went up in a flash. The fire quickly spread to the wood floor and paneling, and pretty soon the whole room was ablaze. That's when Craig and Dana decided to run. But somehow, they got lost in the maze of dark rooms on the second floor, and that's why it took them so long to emerge from the burning building.

Fortunately, the fire only burned a couple of rooms on the second floor. The firefighters' quick response saved the rest of the church. And even more fortunately for our friends, no one ever suspected their involvement in the blaze. None of the chaperones or organizers had seen Craig and Dana slip away from the dance, so they all thought that the fire had started in a faulty electrical socket on the second floor. After all, the church was ancient, and most of the wiring in the place was completely out of date. And given the fact that everything in the church was made of wood, it was like a perfect fire just waiting to happen.

CHAPTER 20

School had finally ended for the year, and we were kicking back and enjoying ourselves.

Craig, Danny, and I were going to the playground every day, playing baseball in the mornings and Ping-Pong and horseshoes in the afternoon. When he could get out of the house, Mike would sometimes join us in the afternoon.

One day shortly before Independence Day, Craig, Danny, and I were walking home after a lazy day of messing around at the playground. Suddenly, a driver in a blue Chevy Impala pulled up behind us and started honking. This was surprising. Although we were now ninth graders and top dogs at Blair Junior High, we still didn't know very many kids who drove.

"Hey guys, it's me!" shouted an all-too-familiar voice. "What's happening?"

Whirling around, the three of us spotted our old bête noire, Todd. His hair was longer and he had grown more facial hair, but he still wore the same thick black Coke-bottle glasses and the same goofy grin on his face.

"Todd," replied Craig carefully. "We're fine. And, how are you?"

"Oh, I'm great. I just decided to look you guys up."

"But where have you been?" asked our leader. "We haven't seen you in forever."

Yeah, and I'd like to keep it that way, I muttered to myself.

None of us was pleased to see Todd again. But now that he'd reappeared, we were all dying to know where he'd been hiding out from the law. He certainly hadn't been hanging out in our area of the world.

"Oh, I've been here and there, enjoying myself!" exclaimed Todd. "But now I'm back here for a day or two, and I just had to see you guys."

Remembering how the police had warned us about him, Craig grew pensive for a moment. He was probably wishing that this apparition that was Todd would just up and disappear. I knew that Danny and I were hoping for the same.

"Well, come on, guys. Show some love to your old buddy," Todd rambled on, trying to rekindle a camaraderie that had never existed. "Why don't you hop into the car so that we can catch up?"

Now, I said to myself, *we're back in the same position as before. But this time there's no way I'm getting into that car.*

"Oh, I don't know about that," protested Craig, searching for some diplomatic way to turn down this unwanted invitation. "We're supposed to be home by five."

"Oh, come on now," responded Todd sarcastically. "You guys are all old enough now to not be so tied to your parents' apron strings. Why in the world do you have to be home by five?"

"So, we can eat dinner."

Now, I'm sure that eating dinner at home was a totally foreign concept to Todd; he probably hadn't eaten a sit-down dinner with his parents since birth. So, his smile turned into a quick sneer. "Eat dinner with your parents? Come on, give me a break. Surely you can skip one dinner at home to hang out with me."

"No," I said, with an unexpected level of firmness. "I really need to get home by five."

"Me, too," added Danny. "I need to get home by five."

Danny's quick refusal surprised me, because he was usually up for anything. But I suspect that all the stories he'd heard from his older brother about Todd had put a damper on even his enthusiasm. Danny liked challenges almost as much as Craig, but he wasn't stupid.

Craig was now the only one left who hadn't responded. Was our leader really considering Todd's invitation? Craig was probably the one Todd most wanted to hang out with. After all, the two of them were kindred spirits—of sorts.

"Well, how about you, Craig?" Todd pressed. "Are you the only friend I have left around here? Or are you too tied to your mama and papa to join me for a drive?"

"I'm not too tied to anyone!" shot back our leader, clearly anxious to demonstrate his independence. Todd certainly knew how to press all the right buttons.

"Well, then, will you come with me?"

"Maybe," replied Craig evenly, like he was stalling for time. "But first I need to know: What do you want to do?"

"Oh, nothing much. We'll just drive around, talk, and drink. And then maybe do something later."

For some strange reason, Craig just couldn't resist this bait. Perhaps he was still fascinated with finding out what made this criminal tick. Or maybe he was just bored with life and the prospect of a long, hot summer stretching ahead. For whatever reason, Craig threw caution to the wind and decided to climb into the blue Chevy with Todd. And so, while he sped off to do "Lord's know-what" with the number-one delinquent in our area, Danny and I headed on home.

Since we were not with Craig that night, it took us a long time to find out what really happened. The next time I saw Craig at the playground, he hemmed and hawed and didn't say much. But over the next week or so, Danny and I managed to pull the full story out of him—or at least what Craig *claimed* was the full story.

He said that the two of them first drove out to the cliffs. Not that Todd had any more alcohol stashed out there, but it was just a good place to talk. This time Todd had all his beer packed into a cooler in the backseat. While they sipped cold Budweisers, Todd started rehashing the usual topics: how much he missed us, how he'd put the manhole cover down all wrong, and how he only cared for his friends.

But Craig showed little or no interest in these stale topics. So, Todd launched into a long tirade about all the people who owed him money in Preston. Five or six people—Craig was never sure exactly how many—owed him over $400. Some of these people had stiffed him when he brought them stolen liquor, and others just owed him from days long past. He wanted desperately to "settle the score" with each and every one of these "delinquents." And that was the real reason he had looked us up. Todd wanted us to serve as lookouts on another one of his demented money-collection forays into Preston.

Craig claimed that he stayed quiet when Todd explained all of this. But our leader must have been worried, real worried. Not only had he been part of Todd's last disastrous excursion into Preston, but this time Craig was all by himself. He didn't have Danny or me to back him up or hide behind.

At some point Todd must have calmed down a bit, because Craig said he eventually tried to reason with him. He claimed that his efforts to drive some sense into this devil-may-care boy went something like this.

"But Todd," he began, "look at what happened last time. The police were waiting for you just as soon as you came out of that house. And they almost caught you."

"Ah hell," Todd objected. "The cops were just lucky to be in the right place at the right time. And I was even luckier, because I got away."

"But aren't you afraid that they'll catch you this time?" Craig pressed. "They're probably on the lookout for you everywhere. And I bet that they have that neighborhood all staked out."

"No, I'm not worried. And anyhow, I need the money," Todd fired back. "I'm really running low on cash."

Being on the run for so long, there was no telling how Todd was getting by. If his dad wasn't helping him, then who was? Surely, he wasn't making much money stealing golf clubs and beer with Grant. The two of them probably couldn't find anyone to buy their clubs, and they probably drank up all the liquor they stole.

After much back and forth with Todd, Craig said that he finally relented. He agreed to accompany Todd back to Preston on one condition: that they visit "only one house." Craig agreed to serve as the silent look-out—nothing more and nothing less.

The two of them drove to a different house in the same shabby part of Preston as before. Craig stayed in the car, while Todd went up to the house. Again, it took a long time for anyone to respond to his loud and insistent knocking. And just like last time, Todd didn't seem to know anyone living in the house. He was only able to worm his way inside after a long and heated discussion with two shaggy people at the door.

It was at this point that Craig's recounting of events grew confused. Craig swore up and down that he never knew that Todd had a gun. But a minute or two after Todd got inside the house, Craig heard gunshots: five or six shots, he said. And then about ten seconds later, Todd came bounding out of the house, running for his life. Leaping into the car, Todd gunned the engine to reverse out of the driveway. But before Todd could get anywhere, someone from inside the house started firing. Several of the shots hit one of the rear tires on the car. So instead of barreling out into the street, the car careened sharply to one side, smashing into a small brick wall between the houses.

"Aw, shit!" yelled Todd, frantically trying to work the gearshift. "I can't get it into reverse!"

With someone still shooting from the house, Todd abruptly abandoned his efforts to get the car moving. "Run!" he screamed. "Run out of the passenger's side, away from the house!"

Craig said that when the shooting started, he crouched down in the well of the front seat of the car. When Todd cried out, he opened the passenger's door, and the two of them tumbled onto the ground. They flattened themselves behind the front wheel of the car while the shots continued to fly.

At this point our leader must have thought he was in some kind of horrible gangster or adventure movie. But this time all the action was for real: the villains in the story were firing at *him*. And he could really get hit and die!

The shooting died down for a moment, and the two of them made a break for it. Crouching low, they ran across the front yard of the next house and then started zigzagging through the backyards of surrounding houses. Fortunately for them, the firing stopped just as soon as they took off. No one came out of the house shooting or chasing after them.

But unfortunately, Todd kept the revolver clasped in his right hand as they ran. So, the two of them must have looked like midnight robbers who were trying to make it off into the night.

Craig never told us where they ran to. He followed Todd, and Todd probably had no idea where he was going. He was only running away from danger, which he was very good at.

When they finally stopped to catch their breath, Todd became quite agitated. He was all worried about the car they'd left behind. "Hell, what are we going to do about the Chevy?" he hollered. "I really need that car to get around. I don't have another set of wheels."

"Can't you just borrow another car?" asked Craig.

"No, I don't know anyone else with a car. And damn, it takes a lot of time to steal another. I really need that Chevy back."

"Can't you just leave it there until morning when things calm down?"

"Hell no! Those guys in that house will hot-wire it and drive it away. I've got to get it back tonight!" yelled Todd.

"That's a crazy idea. Just leave it there until tomorrow."

"Hell no. I need that Chevy back *now*."

"Well, there's no way I'm going back there tonight!" shouted our leader. By now, Craig told us that he had finally had it with Todd's incredibly stupid schemes.

The two of them must have argued about this for quite a while on their way back into Preston. Todd badgered, bullied, and probably even threatened our leader, but Craig remained adamant: he wouldn't return to the house.

Todd must have ditched his gun somewhere along their long walk. By the time they reached the lights of the main street, Todd no longer had the gun in his hand. It also wasn't tucked into his pants. He'd probably thrown it away in the woods.

Craig said he was very relieved to see this. He claimed that at one point Todd got so mad that he was sure he was going to shoot him! Craig even said that Todd had leveled the gun at his head. But I don't believe that story. No way. Craig had a way of embellishing even the strangest of tales—especially when he was relating them to his buddies.

Once they hit the main street, Todd and Craig headed for Chucky's, the popular mom-and-pop store in Preston. Since it was a warm summer night, the usual crowd of young people was hanging in and around the store. So, both boys were soon able to find rides. Todd, still totally obsessed with recovering his car, found a ride back to the scene of the shootout (or at least close to the scene of the shootout). And Craig was able to find a ride back home.

After this wild and unbelievable incident, Todd disappeared. Craig did not see or hear anything more from the fugitive, and neither did we. Even Danny's brother Alan, who usually heard all the latest gossip, had nothing to report. The rumor mill in our town for Todd Banks went completely dry.

According to Craig, Todd never collected on any of his debts in Preston. But he also never got caught for shooting up a house. No neighbors must have reported any gunshots, and no police cruisers must have spotted anything unusual in the bowels of Preston. So, nobody came calling at our doors. It was as if Todd and all the mayhem surrounding his brief visit had never even taken place.

CHAPTER 21

We never did manage to hike to Philadelphia. After his near-death experience on the railroad trestle, Craig abandoned his idea of walking there. While he was always telling us how much fun ultimate physical challenges were, this particular challenge must have put the fear of God into him. Or at least that's the way it seemed to me.

So, I was a bit surprised when in late July our leader came up with yet another Philly-related scheme. This time, instead of hiking to the city, he wanted us to go to Philadelphia International Airport so that we "could watch the planes land." The airport was located maybe seven miles from our homes, not far from the railroad commuter line that had gotten us into so much trouble. So, at first, Craig's idea seemed quite doable. However, as our leader began to spin out his latest idea in more detail, it suddenly became a whole lot more complicated—and dangerous.

"Now, here's what I want to do," he told us one day at the playground. "I want to go up to the airport and then sneak under the fence and get onto the runways."

"Why would we want to do that?" asked Danny, always the critic.

"Because then we can *really* watch the planes land. We'll walk out and lie down on the ground right by the runways. Then the planes will whoosh right over us as they come in to land. Won't that be a scream?"

"What?" cried Danny, grabbing his head like he couldn't believe what he was hearing. "That's a horrible idea! What happens if one of the planes comes down before the runway and hits us on the ground? They wouldn't be able to find all our body parts."

"Aw, don't worry," replied our leader. "The planes *never* touch down before the runway. And anyhow, we'll just be lying on the ground, so there's no way that they could possibly hit us."

"Hell, I'm *not* doing that! Never!" hollered Danny in a very determined voice. "That's the stupidest idea I've ever heard. Where did you ever dream that one up?"

Craig smiled a tight grin before replying with a single word: "Todd."

"What do you mean 'Todd'? Do you want us to do something that idiot did?" Danny was livid. "Look at what he did to you in Preston! Or what he did to all of us on the railroad track!"

"Calm down," soothed Craig, reaching out to touch Danny's shoulder. "Yeah, I got this idea from Todd. When the two of us were drinking beers at the cliffs, he said that he and Grant have gone up to the airport and done this before. If they can do it, why can't we?"

"But those guys are nuts, completely out of their gourd! They do all kinds of insane things that we should never do," I said excitedly. "Just look at what Todd did to you in Preston. It's lucky that you didn't get shot and killed."

"Ah hell, we weren't even close to getting killed," Craig yelled back, talking rapidly like he was trying to convince himself.

"I'm sure glad that I wasn't there," I said.

"Me, too," added Danny.

"Aw hell, you guys just don't get it," replied a now rather frustrated Craig. "Don't you see the thrill we'd get from watching the planes come in just a couple of feet above our heads? It would be a huge rush."

"No!" both of us yelled in unison.

"This is the dumbest idea you've ever had," Danny spat out for good measure. "There's no way I'm ever going to do that."

So that's where Craig's latest scheme ended—for the time being. I myself couldn't believe that he could be stupid enough to want to copy something that Todd had done, especially after the shootout in Preston.

In normal times, Todd and Craig seemed to go their own ways. Whenever Todd appeared on the scene, our leader would usually grow quiet, and a bit defensive. He was always waiting for Todd to screw up, which he did on a regular basis. But deep down, I think that there was a real tension—even rivalry—between the two of them. Since he was not as bright as our leader, Todd may not have recognized this, but I think Craig certainly did. Craig wanted to be just as cool as Todd, but he wanted to use different means. While Todd would try to boss everyone around with his fists, Craig wanted to use the force of his personality. The problem with using personality as a motivator, however, is that sometimes it doesn't work. Craig was more of a moral leader, and those kinds of leaders always have problems getting their buddies to follow along. And Craig certainly wanted us to follow, if only to keep up with Todd.

We didn't hear anything more about this new crazy idea for about a week. Then one day after playing baseball at the playground, Craig announced that Tom, his partner in crime from the homecoming dance, had agreed to "join us" in going to the airport. Now, I have no idea why our leader used the pronoun "us" here, because Danny and I still hadn't agreed to anything. We were still 100 percent opposed to the whole plan. But I do understand why Craig was using his buddy Tom to try to pressure us: Tom the football player was as much a risk-taker as our leader. The main difference between the two of them was that Tom didn't need other people following him around in order to believe in his own self-worth. Tom acted impulsively on his feelings of the moment, whether or not other people wanted to join in. Craig, however, wouldn't move until he had all his cards—or buddies—lined up. From Craig's perspective, inviting the daredevil Tom to join in provided him with another like-minded body to back him up.

In August Craig started to ratchet up the pressure on us. He did this in a new and uncharacteristic way. In the past, Craig would always badger and pester us until we finally gave in. But this time on a quiet Saturday morning at the playground he suddenly declared, "Guess what Tom and I did last night?"

"I give up," Danny replied. "What?"

"We rode the train up to the airport and then snuck in under the fence around the runways. For about half an hour we laid down next to the runway where the planes were coming in. It was so cool!"

"Hell!" shouted Danny. "You guys *are* crazy! Absolutely nuts! Didn't anyone try to stop you?"

Craig flashed his all-knowing grin before replying, "Well, that's why we had to leave. After a while we heard sirens in the distance, and it seemed like they were headed for us. That's when we decided to run back and climb under the fence."

"But wasn't it really scary to watch those huge planes come down just a couple of feet from where you were lying down?" I asked in total disbelief.

"No, like I told you before, it was all very exciting. It was like the mother of all challenges knowing that we were that close to getting smashed! Those planes are incredibly large, and they come in *really* fast!"

"I can't believe the two of you would do that!" shouted Danny, always anxious to get in the last word. "That's just *so* dangerous."

"Aw hell!" replied our leader. "You guys are just a bunch of sissies. You can't spend the rest of the summer playing horseshoes and nimbly-peg at the playground. You've got to get out into the world and try new things. Or else you're just going to be weenies for the rest of your lives!"

The days of summer continued to roll on by, and we carried on with our usual activities. The only change was that Tom started playing baseball with us at the playground. Tom was like Craig, a natural at any sport, so I always wondered why he hadn't joined us before. No doubt Craig now wanted Tom around more in order to get us to act. Whenever the two of them were together, all they talked about was returning to the airport.

"It was so neat being up there on the runway," cooed Craig.

"Just think what it would be like if a whole bunch of us went up there and laid down under the planes," added Tom. "That would be so awesome!"

During these days our younger buddy Mike wasn't much with us. But when he did come down to the playground and heard about the latest adventures of Craig and Tom, he was like us—appalled. Mike was naturally timid, and any scheme like this was just way over the top for him. I think that his misadventures with the dogs in the park and jumping off the cliff had finished him off. He wanted no part of any more of Craig's harebrained schemes.

In mid-August, with the onset of school just around the corner, Craig and Tom became a whole lot more insistent about returning to the airport. They set a Friday night date to return and issued us an ultimatum:

either join them or else they wouldn't play with us for the rest of the sum-mer. This must have been Craig's idea, because Tom would never threaten us like this. In any event, the pressure worked, because a couple of days later, Danny finally relented. "OK, OK. I give up. I'll go with you guys on Friday, but I won't do anything really stupid." For all his outward bluster, I suspect that Danny just couldn't bear the thought of spending the rest of the summer without Craig.

"So, what about you, Sonny?" asked Craig, turning his steely blue eyes on me. "Are you going to come?"

"Aw hell!" I moaned, feeling like a cornered animal. "If Danny's going, I guess that I have to come, too." I was just as afraid of spending the rest of the summer without Craig as Danny must have been. Danny and I related more to Craig than to each other, and without Craig, things would've just been hopeless for me. He was my best buddy.

On the appointed Friday night, the four of us met at the railroad sta-tion and took the train up to the airport. On the ride, Craig and Tom chat-tered away like little kids headed for the first time to the beach. They were really excited. Danny and I, however, were quiet and much more apprehen-sive. We had absolutely no idea what we were getting ourselves into.

At the airport station we followed Craig up the stairs and toward the terminal. But just when the terminal appeared straight ahead, Craig had us turn right along a sidewalk that circled the airport. The sidewalk headed out toward a long-term parking lot. About halfway to the lot, Craig pointed out an embankment to our right. We scampered up the hill and then scooted through a small hole in the fence. Now we were right near the runways and could see the service trucks shuttling back and forth between the planes. In the distance we could also see planes taking off and landing.

"There are so many planes and runways around here," said Danny. "How do we know where to go?"

"Don't worry," replied our leader. "Just follow me."

And so, we ran from one runway to another, staying crouched down all the time in order to avoid the sweeping lights of the various service vehicles. We scooted around like this for maybe half a mile, always staying down, until we were a long way from the terminal. Then Craig announced, "Here's the one. Let's lie down just before this runway."

"But it all looks so scary," I shouted, frightened out of my wits. "How do we know if this is the right one? If they're taking off from this runway, they're sure to hit us on the way up."

"Shut up, and don't worry," blazed Craig, behaving more like Todd now. "I know what I'm doing. This is definitely a landing runway: you can tell by the color of the lights. Come on now and lie down here in the grass like me and Tom."

So, we all laid down right by the runway. Being the foolhardiest of the group, Craig and Tom positioned themselves closest to the runway, the beginning of which was marked by a series of long white lines. Danny and I settled down in the grass a bit farther away. Except for the small white lights marking the position of the runway, it was as dark as Hades.

It didn't take very long for the first plane to swoop in and land right over us. We could spot it coming from a long way away; it descended through the darkness with landing gear deployed and lights ablaze. Actually, the first plane we spotted like this landed at an adjacent runway. But the second one, coming in about five minutes later, came in to land on the runway where we were at. It landed maybe twenty feet over us. The plane was unbelievably large and noisy; we had to cover our ears tightly to keep from going deaf.

"Woo-wee!" yelled Craig as soon as the huge plane had cleared us and touched down on the runway. "Wasn't that wonderful? It's mind-blowing how close these planes come to you out here. What a thrill!"

I looked at Danny, and he stared back glass-eyed at me. Neither of us had anything to say. It was definitely exciting, but it was also very, very scary. A slight miscalculation by the pilot here or there, and we would've been goners in a second.

Three other planes followed and landed right over us. The planes seemed to come in at regularly spaced five- or ten-minute intervals. They also seemed to alternate between our runway and the one right next to us. We could spot all the planes coming into land for a mile or two away in the pitch-black sky. Starting out like tiny pinpricks of light, they'd grow larger and larger until they became these huge, deafening behemoths swooping in right over us.

By the time the fifth plane approached our runway, Craig and Tom had decided to move from the grass onto the edge of the runway itself. I have no idea what impelled them to do this; maybe they were looking for more thrills. They never signaled their move to us. Danny and I were still lying immobilized in the grass a short distance from the runway. We had no desire to move anywhere except back home.

The fifth plane seemed to take the same landing approach as the others. But in the last quarter mile or so, something seemed wrong, at least to me. The plane was too loud or too low or too something; its trajectory just felt different from the others. Danny and I covered our ears as it descended, but even that wasn't enough to prevent us from hearing a loud, double thud as the plane flew in over us.

The thuds sent an ominous chill down our spines. As soon as the plane touched down on the runway, we jumped up and started running to where we had last seen our buddies.

"Craig! Tom! Where are you? Are you OK?"

No reply. And so, we frantically began searching around for them in the pitch black. We saw no sign of them at the end of runway; nor was there any sign of them anywhere near the runway. Finally, we spotted what looked like two clumps of clothing lying some thirty yards off the runway.

"Craig! Tom! Are you guys OK? This is no time for stupid games!" we shouted, sprinting toward the clothing. "Get up and show us that you're OK!"

Again, no response.

Danny was the first to reach the clothing.

"Oh shit!" he screamed, jumping away in horror. "This is *horrible,* absolutely horrible. They're both all bloody and beaten up. And they sure look dead to me."

We carefully turned our friends over. Danny was right: they looked absolutely terrible, like they had both been smashed and tossed by a huge Mack truck. Their faces were all bloody and black-and-blue, almost unrecognizable. Their arms and legs were torn up and twisted in impossible angles.

"Oh my God!" I cried, throwing my hands to the sky. "Shit! This is terrible, just terrible! How could this *ever* happen?"

Maybe our buddies had tried to sit up or stand as the plane came in. Or maybe the plane came in too low and the landing gear was too close to the ground. In any event, Craig and Tom were now dead. Very dead. And we had to face the consequences.

CHAPTER 22

Maybe Danny and I should have run. But where could we have run to? Our leader and one of his good friends were now dead. So where could we possibly flee?

Danny and I started screaming and crying. And we probably yelled every cussword in the book. And then we did run, yelling and sobbing the whole way. But instead of running away, this time we headed right for the terminal. We ran over and around the runways until we spotted a police car parked next to the terminal. And there we spilled the beans to two young policemen sitting in their cruiser.

"Officer! Officer!" shouted Danny, who was the first to arrive. "We need help! We were lying out by the runways and some planes hit two of our friends. And now they're dead."

"Whoa, whoa, slow down, kid," ordered the officer, totally amazed to see two distraught teenagers come running up to his car from the runways. "Slow down and tell me the whole story. Where were you, and what were you doing?"

"There were four of us, and we were lying out by the runways to watch the planes land," Danny yelled, spitting out his words in rapid fire.

"And then something terrible happened, and one of the planes must have hit our friends, and now they're lying out there dead."

"Where's 'out there,' kid?" the cop asked, arching his eyebrows as he tried to make sense of this unbelievable story.

"There!" said Danny, pointing in the direction of the runways.

The two policemen looked at each other in total disbelief. They probably thought we were liars or lunatics—or worse. But then the one in the driver's seat, who seemed to be in charge, asked slowly but emphatically, "Kid, are you *sure* that you're telling us the truth?"

"Yes, officer. I'm telling the truth."

With this, the two officers jumped into action. The driver got on his radio, while the other one leaped out and shoved us into the back of the cruiser.

"Airport command," barked the driver into his radio. "We've got a possible 999 on runway 01-005. Request permission to investigate."

"Permission granted," replied a disemboweled voice from nowhere.

"Also request permission to activate all-hands notice."

"Permission granted."

"OK, kid," said the driver, turning to us in the back, "show us the exact spot where you last saw your friends."

Through our tears, we did our best to direct him back to the place. As we started driving, all hell broke loose at the airport. Sirens began to wail, and fire trucks and ambulances suddenly appeared, racing out of the terminal. All of them followed us in a line out onto the tarmac.

When we reached the place where we thought our friends were, an older sergeant in a following car took over. He had us get out of the cruiser and show him where the bodies laid. And then he escorted us right back to the cruiser. It was like he was afraid that we might take off.

It took the medics, firemen, and policemen about half an hour to mark off the scene of the accident and to recover the remains of our friends. They carried the bodies—covered with white sheets—back on stretchers to a waiting ambulance. During this whole time, we sat in the back of the cruiser in tears and total disbelief.

Once this was over, the sergeant returned to the car and began firing all kinds of questions at us: "What are your names? What are the names of your buddies? Was anyone else with you tonight? Whose idea was this? Was this the first time you did this? How did you get onto the runways? How close were you to the airplanes? How come your friends got hit and you didn't?"

Danny did most of the talking; I only helped to fill in the gaps. We answered in brief, short monotones and did our best to answer truthfully. But sometimes we stumbled over questions like, "Whose idea was this?" We didn't want to implicate Todd in this tragedy for fear that he would somehow come back and get us. So, we just said that it was Craig's idea, which was kind of true. To the question, "Was this the first time you did this?" we both replied yes. Of course, that was true for the two of us, but not so true for Craig and Tom. We figured that what the cops didn't know wouldn't hurt them.

The sergeant and the others appeared to be especially interested in our answer to the question: "Why did your friends get hit and you didn't?" They must have asked us different variations of this question about twenty times. We gave the best response we could: "They were looking for more thrills than we were." It didn't seem right to say that they were braver than we were. It also didn't seem right to say that they were more foolhardy. Both of us knew that it's wrong to speak ill of the dead.

Danny and I sobbed throughout the questioning. Danny tried his best to stop crying, but every time I looked over, his eyes were filled with tears and his face was red as a beet. And all night long he replied in short, clipped sentences that just weren't his style. In normal times, Danny usually rambled on and on.

The worst moment of the night came after the police drove us back to the station. There they called Craig's and Tom's parents and asked them to come down and identify the bodies. I'll never forget watching Craig's shell-shocked parents as they filed past us at the station. The withering, hate-filled look that his mom gave me is something that I will take to my grave.

Neither Danny nor I attended the memorial services and funerals that followed. What was the point? At best, our presence would only have reminded everyone of the incredibly stupid thing we'd done. At worst, someone might have decided to take out their anger on us. After all, how was anyone to know who was the cause of this horrible tragedy?

Danny and I didn't see too much of each other in the days after the accident. The two of us weren't nearly as close as each of us was to Craig. Our parents also pressured each of us to stay away from each other. Each set of parents seemed convinced that the other boy was the evil Frankenstein who had dreamed up this nefarious act. What did they know?

For some strange reason this time my parents didn't hit or punish me. They didn't even ground me. But they did make me sit down for several heart-to-heart talks about life and death and taking responsibility.

"Do you know that it's wrong to take a life? Even when it's not entirely your fault?" they would begin.

But I would have no answer.

"And that you have to take responsibility for *all* your actions? Even for those actions that you don't entirely embrace."

Again, I stayed silent.

My parents also made me go see the minister. I had about as much to say to him as to my parents. With my parents it was just too difficult to explain how I got involved in the whole mess, and with the minister, well, I just didn't know him that well. And really, what was there to say? I'd made a dreadful mistake by following Craig. I should have put my foot down. I should have tried harder to convince him not to go.

I pretty much moped around the house the rest of August. With Craig no longer around and an unofficial ban on seeing Danny, I really had no friends in town. I also had no reason to go to the playground. I was sure that everyone down there was going around whispering, "Did you hear what happened at the airport?" and I had no desire to be the object of such gossip. That would've been way too embarrassing.

The only person who called me during this whole time was Mike. I was really surprised to hear his voice. I bet his mom made him call, because he didn't have much to say.

"Hi, Sonny," he began. "How are you doing?"

"Not so great," I replied in all honesty.

"Mm, do you want to get together and do something?"

"No, not right now. Maybe later."

"OK."

And that was that.

I can't blame Mike; he was trying his best. He was still in the dark about many things. He didn't know anything about the accident on the railroad tracks, and he didn't know much about our trip to the airport. He knew that Craig and Tom had been pressuring us to go, but that's all. He knew nothing about why Craig and Tom got hit by that plane, and I didn't, either.

In a way, Mike's timidity had served him well. He hadn't been a part of either of our gang's greatest disasters.

I must admit that I had my share of nightmares during those final weeks before school began in September. My nightmares were all the same: Craig and I would be on the train headed for the airport. I don't know where our other buddies were, but this time Craig and I were alone. And we were having all the fun. I'd thrown caution to the wind, and the two of us were laughing and carrying on about how great it was going to be to lie down in the grass near the runways. It was going to be the thrill of a lifetime.

In my nightmares, I was no longer the silent follower; instead, I was step for step with Craig. Actually, at the airport I was the first one to scamper under the fence, and I was also the one to lead us to the runway. I don't know what got into my head, but in my nightmares, I became just like Craig: bossy and fearless and completely determined. Out on the tarmac I was the one who urged that we move closer to the edge of the runway. And I was the one who suggested that we go and actually lie right down on the runway.

And so, guess what? When that monstrous plane came in to land a little too close to the ground, guess who was the one who got hit? Me. And not Craig. So, it was me who was lying on the ground, and Craig who was left wondering where to run.

But I've never been able to decide what it's like to be dead. Therefore, I always woke up at this point, sweating and all twisted up in the sheets. But at least I was still alive.

I have no idea what my nightmares meant. Maybe they were trying to tell me how close I came to death. Or maybe they were painting the dangers of being a take-charge, invincible leader. Or maybe they were demonstrating the fine line between courage and stupidity. I don't know. My nightmares bothered me a lot, but I didn't dare share them with anyone.

I was relieved when school finally resumed in early September. At last I had something to do and I could escape reliving the events of the airport disaster in my head. And my classmates were actually pretty understanding: none of them asked me about what happened, and I never heard any of them whispering behind my back. Of course, I did notice some kids in the hall pointing at me. But I could live with that.

What I couldn't understand was why Mr. Fagan, the no-nonsense vice principal, singled me out again for special treatment. The second week of school, he summoned Danny and me to another "sitting down" in his office.

"Hi there, Sonny and Danny," he began, smiling ominously. "Did the two of you have a pleasant summer?"

"Yes, sir," replied Danny, in a weak and strained voice.

"Did you do anything exciting?"

Now, I'm sure that Mr. Fagan knew all the details about our escapade at the airport. And I'm equally sure that he wanted the two of us to tell him all about it. That way he could lull us into a kind of false comradery whereby he could extract details of other past evil deeds from our heads. At least that's the way they did it in the movies, and I'm sure that Mr. Fagan was a big fan of the cinema.

But Danny and I were having no part of this sneaky scheme. So, I quickly replied for the two of us, "No, nothing much happened."

"Oh," replied the sour disciplinarian, a bit taken back. "Are you sure? How about your other friends? By any chance did you see Todd Banks this summer?"

"No, sir," replied Danny, lying halfway. While he had certainly seen Todd in the summer, Danny hadn't had anything to do with him. It was Craig who had gone off with Todd in the car in July, and now Craig was no more.

"So, you don't know about his whereabouts? Or anything more about his involvement in that terrible railroad accident that killed one person?"

"No, sir."

Our interview session continued on in fits and starts. Although Mr. Fagan wheedled this way and that, he got no useful information out of us. Since we'd already met with the authorities about the airport tragedy, and the police still had no suspicions about our involvement in anything else, Mr. Fagan could not exactly give us detention.

In the end he had to reluctantly let us go with a warning: "Now, boys, you and I both know that the details about that railroad accident have never been fully resolved. So, if you ever want to come and talk to me about that incident or anything else, my door is always open."

I knew Mr. Fagan had his suspicions about us. And he just couldn't let them go.

CHAPTER 23

My world pretty much ended when Craig died. I had no one to follow around after school or on the weekends. I thought about trying out for the ninth-grade football team; that certainly would've given me something to do. But when I heard that Danny only made the second-string team, I knew that it would be hopeless. I'd be lucky to even make the team.

Fortunately, Mike came up to me in the hall one day and suggested that we start walking to school together. Maybe his mom put him up to this, too. But it was a nice gesture that I accepted right on the spot. I was lonely and really needed a pal.

I don't know where Danny was around this time. We both would've loved for him to join us on our daily walks to school. Danny was fun and adventurous and full of all sorts of good ideas. But probably his parents were still warning him to stay away from me, the "bad boy." And once Danny started playing on the ninth-grade team, he began hanging out with a whole different crowd.

"So, do you want to get together this weekend?" I asked Mike on the first Friday we walked to school. I was trying to cast myself in Craig's role here: that of organizing the troops for Saturday. But I didn't have anything planned; I really just wanted to get out of the house.

"Sure," replied Mike, in an eager voice. "What do you want to do?"

"How about if we go down to the park and see if anyone's playing football? If they are, we can join in."

But when we arrived at the playground that Saturday, no one was playing football. A few boys were shooting hoops, but neither of us wanted to play basketball.

Searching for something else to do, I suggested, "How about if we hike in the woods?" It was a gorgeous fall day, and the leaves were just beginning to change.

"Sure, why not? But let's stay away from the cliffs. They didn't treat me very well."

To avoid the cliffs, we began to walk south through the woods. We usually didn't head in this direction, because it was away from Preston and Philadelphia. But we didn't care; all we wanted to do was to rustle through the leaves and throw rocks at squirrels. And there were plenty of squirrels scurrying about, stocking up on acorns for the winter.

Pretty soon we came upon another place that held bad memories for Mike: the fenced-in park.

"Oh hell!" he shouted. "I totally forgot that this damn park was this way." Neither of us had been anywhere near this mystery place since Mike had been bitten by that dog.

"Shit," he continued, as we skirted along the high barbed-wired fence. "I can't believe that I let Craig talk me into climbing that fence and then searching around for secret agents. I knew it was a dumber-than-dumb idea, but I still did it. What the hell was I thinking?"

"I think that you wanted to win the ten-dollar bet," I suggested diplomatically.

"No, that had nothing to do with it," he snapped. "I just didn't want to get kicked out of the gang."

"Oh, yeah. I forgot that Craig threatened you with that."

"Craig could really be mean, especially when he wanted to pressure you to do one of his schemes. And the dumber the idea, the more he pushed."

"Why do you think he was like that?" I asked, wondering out loud how other people viewed our late leader's motivations.

"I think that he was kind of insecure," Mike responded, after a bit of thought. "Insecure because he always wanted a bunch of guys following him around. And insecure because he was always trying to keep up with Todd and Grant."

This insight really surprised me. I'd never heard anyone talk like this. Especially not Mike, the most reserved member of our gang. When the four of us were together, I'd say little, and Mike would say even less.

"Do you really think so?" I asked, anxious to hear more of his thoughts before he clammed up again.

"Sure—sure I do. Craig was always dreaming up these cockamamie plans to see who would follow him and who wouldn't. And the plans got more screwed up the more he wanted to keep up with the bad boys. Craig was basically a good guy who liked to show off, but when he got around those hooligans, he just lost his bearings and became a menace."

"A menace? How do you mean?" I asked, puzzled.

"I don't know," Mike replied, biting his lip as he thought. "Maybe more of a threat or a danger, than a menace."

"A threat to himself or to everyone?"

"Oh, for sure, to everyone," Mike said without a moment's hesitation. "Look at the way he led you guys to the airport. There he was just trying to keep up, or maybe even surpass, Todd. Todd could only get Grant to go with him up there, but Craig got three of you suckers to follow."

"Do you really think that we were suckers?" I asked, a little taken back.

"Sure, suckers or worse."

I let all of this sink in for a minute before venturing, "So, why do you think we all followed him around?"

"I don't know. I suppose that in the beginning his ideas were neat and exciting. I mean, who makes their friends crawl through a smelly old sewer pipe to win a bet about rats? Or who sneaks alcohol into a school dance after all the school administrators have repeatedly warned us not to? We had nothing else to do, so it was fun to follow along and see what would happen. And to see what idiotic plan he would dream up next."

"But you weren't there on his craziest schemes," I countered. "You were always leaving us to go home."

"Yeah, after I got bitten, I decided it was best to avoid his stupidest challenges," Mike responded, with considerable conviction. "And they really did get dumber as time progressed. But I sure did hear how they all turned out from you guys."

"And you weren't there for Craig's worst idea: going to the airport."

"No," Mike said, choosing his words carefully. "By that time, I knew that he was way too much under the influence of Todd and Grant. And his ideas just weren't fun anymore—they were more deadly and dangerous than anything else."

"I wish that I could've seen that, too."

"Yeah, that would've been nice."

ABOUT THE AUTHOR

RICHARD H. ADAMS, JR. has lived in Pennsylvania, California, and Virginia. He worked as a poverty researcher for the World Bank and other international organizations in Washington, DC. He has also taught at the University of California, Berkeley, Princeton University, and Georgetown University. This is his fifth book and first novel.